Julie Goldbucket

J.D. Pujals

Contents

Dedication

To you, dear readers, whose curiosity and search for deeper truths have given life to these pages. May this adventure alongside Julie Goldbucket inspire you to explore your own labyrinths of self-discovery and spirituality. May you find in this story the courage to accept simplicity and the strength to let go of what no longer serves you. In every corner of nature and in every meaningful relationship, may you find the answers you seek and the peace you deserve. This is a story of transformation and the power of human connections; may it accompany you on your own path to a life of happiness and absolute fulfillment.

Acknowledgements

To my beloved cat, whose constant companionship has enriched my everyday life with happiness and unconditional affection, teaching me the essence of eternal love. To my chosen family and dear friends, the lights that illuminate my path.

To the majestic nature and the breathtaking beauty of our planet, which have always been a source of inspiration, satiating my spirit and enriching my soul with every sunrise.

To the vast universe, with its profound mysteries and splendid wonders, for the lessons and blessings it offers us. In every star in the sky, in every breath of wind, and in every beat of my heart, I have found the magic and wisdom I had always sought.

To the readers, may your curiosity and passion for exploring new adventures bring these pages to life. May this literary adventure transport you to a world full of imagination and reflection and provide you with answers to those questions that accompany us on this journey of existence.

About the Author

J.D. Pujals (born May 16, 1984, in Santo Domingo, Dominican Republic) is a multifaceted Canadian artist. Renowned as a painter, sculptor and writer, his work reflects a fusion of the figurative and the abstract, infused with a mystical touch and a deep connection with nature.

From an early age, he showed an innate inclination toward art and writing, exploring the intersections between the human mind, the universe, and magic. His literary style, inspired by Latin American magical realism, is characterized by its relaxed, casual, and lighthearted tone, which invites internal reflection and the search for each individual's purpose in life.

J.D. Pujals' educational and professional background is as diverse as his art. At the age of 6, he moved to the United States, where he was exposed to a new culture and outlook on life. This early experience enriched his worldview and contributed to the formation of his artistic identity. Subsequently, he returned to the Dominican Republic to continue his studies. He graduated with a degree in advertising, a discipline that, along with his exposure to Dominican culture, influenced his understanding of visual communication and storytelling, aspects that he would later integrate into his art.

Following his training in advertising, he ventured to Chile, where the region's rich cultural diversity and artistic effervescence further stimulated his creativity. He decided to study industrial design in Spain, thus exploring new aesthetic and conceptual dimensions that would be reflected in his work. After completing his training, he returned from Spain to Chile, where he worked as a teacher of English as a second language for several years, working for one of the largest pharmaceutical companies in the world.

He later moved to Canada, where he currently lives. He is deeply influenced by the landscapes, cultural diversity, and society's commitment to environmental protection and animal rights. This experience marked a significant change in his life, leading him to adopt a plant-based lifestyle, which he incorporates into his writings through a strong message of environmental awareness and respect for all forms of life.

His art has been exhibited and recognized internationally, highlighting its ability to evoke emotions and awaken people's imagination. His commitment to exploring the human soul and promoting happiness and fulfillment is reflected in both his art and his words, demonstrating that the true purpose of life lies in living in harmony with oneself and the world around us.

J.D. Pujals' work transcends borders and cultures, inspiring others to seek beauty and meaning in every moment of life and the magic all around us.

Epigraph

"Beneath the surface of societal expectations lies the absolute power to find our true purposes. In the exploration of self-discovery, we must learn to let go of distractions and listen to the whispers of nature. There we will be able to discover the secrets of a life full of happiness and satisfaction..."

Preface

In this world we share, fast-paced life and luxuries seem to be the epitome of success. Sometimes we forget to pause and reflect on what really matters. This fantastic narrative is steeped in unconventional wisdom that will transport you to a world full of mysteries and invite you to reflect through the life of Julie Goldbucket, a woman who thrives in the business world in the northwest of the Pacific Ocean.

To the naked eye Julie's life may seem like the embodiment of perfection, with a privileged position in a high-profile company, a loving fiancé, and great financial success, but beneath the surface, Julie was searching for the true meaning of life and discovering the authenticity of her own being. This story explores the delicate balance between ambition and inner fulfillment, offering an intimate insight into the search for clarity, purpose, and happiness.

The amazing adventure is born with a series of unexpected events and unusual encounters that challenge Julie's perception of reality and the conventional path she had always known. As she navigates through the enigmatic messages of her dreams, the guidance of her beloved father, and the unconventional wisdom of her best friend, Maple, Julie begins to question her desires and redefine her priorities.

This story invites you to explore themes of personal growth, spirituality, mental health, and the power of human connections. Julie's experience can resonate with any human being who has ever felt trapped by social expectations or questioned the value of a life built solely on ambition.

Introduction

This is a story of transformation, where the search for success collides with the mysteries of the human spirit. Julie Marie Goldbucket, a motivated marketing professional, is on a journey of self-discovery, challenged by the cosmic forces of the universe. As the pace of life threatens to devour her, Julie is met with a series of unusual messages, mystical encounters, and profound life lessons. This is the story of Julie's quest for absolute power, a journey that takes her from the top of the corporate world to the heart of nature, from love to personal reinvention, where she learns that with every challenge comes the power to shape her destiny. Join Julie on this moving odyssey that mixes the mundane with the mystical, in a tale that whispers: "All answers await you in nature".

Chapter 1: Juggling

The rustling of paper bags announced Julie's arrival from the store. She had picked up a bag of frozen berries, another step in her conversion to a healthier vegetarian lifestyle. It had been three years since she made the switch, inspired by her best friend Maple, who was already a full-fledged vegan, though perhaps the most important reason was her love for her cat. Julie couldn't even begin to imagine her cat suffering like the animals in the food industry suffer. It didn't make sense to call herself an animal lover and also eat them. It was simply unethical in every sense of the word. Julie was proud of the jump to vegetarian. The goal, without a doubt, was to be vegan like Maple, but, as her mother used to tell her, step by step.

After making herself a smoothie, Julie settled into her luxurious emerald green velvet sectional sofa, and her loving cat, Bagel, climbed on top of her and began purring. Bagel's vibration and the sound of her music from the kitchen speakers, a playlist of pop hits from the early 2000s, was certainly comforting. Her taste in music was nothing extraordinary, but it was the soundtrack of her life. Julie closed her eyes and let those songs from better times flood her mind, while allowing a small smile to form at the corners of her mouth. Suddenly, the only "Gleeter" song she liked came on, and Julie turned up the volume.

Julie was one of those rare souls who exuded kindness even when the world drove her insane. She couldn't help but offer a friendly smile to anyone, even those she disliked. It was simply her nature.

Television wasn't exactly her favorite pastime, but she occasionally tuned in to the news channel to stay informed. Although she didn't like to admit it, she loved politics. Her intimate moments with the TV usually happened in her comfortable and rather expensive bed. Her mattress was probably the most expensive thing she had in her luxurious penthouse. Julie and Sam, her fiancé, had the guilty pleasure of watching beauty pageants together.

Julie's weekend rituals often involved her best friend, Maple. "Girls' nights" were almost always at Maple's. There was a lot of laughter, chatter about life, love, work, and everything in between. They always watched their favorite show: "Race for Fashion"; that allowed them to forget life's problems for at least a moment. Bagel, used to make a cameo when girls' night happened at Julie's house. His lazy and always hungry nature held a special place in their hearts. Oh, and Julie's favorite Carmenere wine, pistachios, cashews, and plant-based sweet and sour gummies couldn't be missing.

Every morning, Bagel meowed at Julie at a terribly inconvenient hour. No meow could wake her from her sleep before 6:00 a.m., even if he had been meowing incessantly since 5:00. a.m. Julie cherished every second she could stay in bed, stealing a little extra time before having to face the stressful day that generally awaited her.

Julie was juggling a super demanding job at one of the largest multinational marketing agencies in the world. Her prominent position was the result of many years of tireless work and dedication. She was about to become partner, or at least that was what the voices in the office murmured.

But her success came at a cost, a heavy one that she was determined not to show the world.

With wedding plans to deal with and an exorbitant amount of responsibilities, Julie's life was like a water balloon stuck to a hose, about to explode and leave everything soaked. Stress and anxiety were escalating, but Julie couldn't afford to show her vulnerability, not now.

Julie sighed as she looked at the clock. The digital numbers on her designer watch flashed at 9:09 p.m., reminding her that her peaceful night was quickly fading away. With her work responsibilities and a wedding on the way, seconds felt like precious particles of sand slipping through her fingers in the wind.

She reluctantly decided to get off the couch, knowing that she had to prepare for the day ahead. The ridiculous overload of work wouldn't wait for her and her dedication was the reason she was climbing the corporate ladder at such a rapid pace. She gently patted Bagel on the back a few times to make him move, and she got up from the couch. As she walked to the bathroom to brush her teeth, she couldn't help but glance at the wedding planning magazines that were scattered around the coffee table. Julie thought of her mom Dinorah's crazy idea to hire the pop star: "Gleeter" for her wedding party. She didn't even like Gleeter, but the idea of meeting the superstar made her a little excited. Gleeter had had a couple of hits in the 2000s but struggled with addiction and had a couple of horrible relationships that had given her, her three children. Then she disappeared from the public spotlight for years, but recently she had made her comeback to fame, thanks to the super successful show "Race for Fashion", which she began to host. She then released a new album for the first time in years, and this one was extremely successful, selling millions of copies and filling stadiums around the world. People began to call her "the zombie of pop". Because she came back from the dead.

Julie used to spend an excessive amount of time brushing her teeth, a useless attempt to take away the taste of stress that had lodged in the back of her mouth. Honestly, there wasn't even time for a quiet cup of coffee in the morning, but Julie couldn't resist a quick stop at the trendy coffee shop that charged an outrageous $12 for her beloved Mokafakachino with oat "milk." When she arrived at work, her routine was like a well-greased clock. Almost every day, she was on time, a feat accomplished with meticulous precision. Julie wasn't just a consultant; She was one of the best in the business, and her reputation had spread like fire in a pine forest in the wind. In her office, awards and certificates filled the walls and shelves, clear proof of her expertise and sacrifice.

But it wasn't just her career that made her spin plates like a juggler from a Chinese circus. Julie was planning her wedding to Sam. They had been engaged for what seemed like an eternity, and every detail had to be absolutely perfect. The guest list, the flowers, the venue, the configuration of the tables, the photography, the videography, everything; It was an endless to-do list that seemed to grow like poisonous weed.

That same night, with a deep sigh, she turned on her computer in the office on the second floor of her penthouse and prepared for another demanding day the next morning. She was just a cup of expensive coffee, from diving headfirst into the tsunami of things to do. But it was too late. Julie knew that if she drank coffee at night, she wouldn't be able to sleep at all. Not sleeping, although quite common, was the worst thing that could happen to her in her busy life.

Julie's life was an impressive balancing act and with every breath, she teetered on the edge of an abyss. As she checked her emails and tackled the day's tasks, thoughts of all the juggling she was doing were crowding in her mind and she couldn't help but wonder how much longer she could keep all the plates in balance without them all smashing on the floor and shattering into a thousand pieces.

Julie's computer screen was filled with charts, reports, and emails, each demanding her immediate attention, as always. As she immersed herself in her work, her mind swam in thoughts of her wedding getting closer and closer, the struggle to become a partner in the agency, and on top of that, everything that was happening at once in her busy life.

She knew there was no time to hesitate. Her dreams of becoming a partner at Irguitzu Marketing Ltd. and the promise of a beautiful life alongside Sam depended on her total commitment.

Julie looked at the clock and realized that it was already past 10:00 p.m. The music on her playlist was still playing in the kitchen; a Korean pop song by the group "Vanilla Cherry". However, peace seemed far away. Fatigue weighed heavily on her shoulders, but she couldn't let anyone notice.

With one last sip of her berry smoothie, Julie immersed herself back in her work, fully aware that her life was simply stressful and there was nothing she could do about it. There were challenges ahead, but Julie always found a way to face them with the same grace and strength that had carried her so high.

Chapter 2: I'm Going Insane!

Julie's fingers glided agilely over the cracked screen of her latest-model Pineapple phone, as she dialed her friend Maple's number. She needed a lifeline for the sea of stress she was drowning in. Today would be her first opportunity to close the deal for the great Latin American campaign. Her optimism was high; she believed that everything would turn out in her favor, the key to her long-awaited promotion.

Maple's voice sounded reassuring on the other end of the line. "Hey Julie, what's up?"

Julie let out a sigh, the weight of her stress slumping on her shoulders. "Maple, I'm going insane! The promotion, the wedding, the account for the Latin American market, Sam, everything!" Her voice trembled as she poured out her fears and anxieties.

Maple listened intently, her presence reassuring Julie over the phone. "Julie, take a deep breath, count to ten. You can do this; you know you can! You've worked like a maniac for that promotion and you're not alone, I'll always be by your side. You will succeed in everything; the wedding, the Latin American account and everything else. Remember, you will always have me by your side, even if you don't want to."

Julie's eyes filled with tears. Maple's unwavering support was like a remedy for her exhausted soul. She blinked and pulled herself together. "I know, Maple. It's just that sometimes, it feels like I'm trying to spin too many plates at once and I feel like I'm going to drop them all."

Maple let out a small chuckle, her voice full of warmth saying, "Well, remember I'm here to help you catch those plates when they're about to fall off. And speaking of which, why don't you take a deep breath, finish your break, face what's left of the day like you always have, and then let's go out to dinner or something tonight? It's girls' night and we can talk about our problems together."

Julie's shoulders relaxed at the thought of spending time with her best friend. "You're the best, Maple. I don't know what I would do without you."

As they continued to chat, Julie felt her anxiety melt away. She knew she had an ally in Maple, a partner in her personal life and her great support in her professional life, who would be there to celebrate her victories and to help her carry her heaviest burdens.

Julie ended the call and prepared to face the second half of her day with her head held high. The Latin American account, the promotion, the wedding, and everything else was still a challenge, but for now, the important thing was to get through the day.

It was time for the first meeting with Mr. Ramón Chespirito, who was the executive director of the "Verypech" brand of cuaba soap. Mr. Chespirito was known to be very gallant with women and had a weakness for voluptuous women with curly hair, such as Julie Goldbucket was. Julie entered the meeting room where there were only three women, one of them being the secretary of the CEO of Irguitzu Marketing Ltd., Mr. Thomas Woodfire.

Mr. Chespirito, trying to be funny, said: 'I thought this was a Marketing agency, not a Modeling agency!' Julie felt super uncomfortable, but she smiled, and fake laughed. Mr. Woodfire could only roll his eyes and tried to start the meeting as soon as possible. Julie came well prepared. The work at home was worth it.

Benjie, Julie's assistant, had everything ready to start. And the presentation was a resounding success. Mr. Chespirito seemed impressed, but the truth seemed that, rather than the presentation, it was because of Julie's appearance. He then left and Julie stayed for a moment with Thomas Woodfire, his secretary Grisell and one of the partners, a bootlicker named Joan.

Mr. Woodfire asked to speak to Julie alone. Joan, of course, tried to stay with them, but Woodfire insisted that he wanted to talk to Miss Goldbucket alone. When the two of them were alone, Julie felt super intimidated, the truth was that Mr. Woodfire was super handsome, with his well-tidied hair and his perfect gray beard. Julie was attentive to see what Woodfire wanted, and he tells her: Julie, I won't beat around the bush, your promotion depends entirely on this account. "As you know, saving the environment is quite expensive and I need all the money I can get, and Mr. Chespirito, although nouveau riche, is quite rich and I need his money."

Julie didn't know what to say about it. But the truth is that it didn't matter. She had worked for this all her career and now it was at her fingertips. She could almost taste victory.

Chapter 3: The Goldbucket Family

Julie's family had instilled in her the values of hard work and dedication. In her home, there was no concept of giving up. For her parents, marriage was a lifelong commitment, and work was fundamental to achieving success in life. It was not about achieving work-life balance; It was about making everything work, no matter how many plates you had to keep spinning.

Her quality education had instilled in her the idea that she had to excel at everything, all the time. It was a standard she clung to mercilessly. The pressure was relentless, but she carried it like armor.

Julie's family expected certain things from her, and marrying Sam was one of them. It was not an "option"; she loved Sam very much, and they had been together since high school. He was a successful, wealthy lawyer, and he was also Jewish, earning him the unreserved approval of her mother Dinorah.

As Julie sat at her desk, surrounded by a mountain of papers and responsibilities, her thoughts drifted to the uncertainty that had been bothering her for years. There was something about Sam that didn't quite fit into her meticulously organized life.

While she knew Sam loved her, she couldn't help but wonder if she was in love with him. Her mind circled and struggled to find clarity amid the chaos of her thoughts.

The demands of her job, the forms to fill out, the papers to sign, the memos to write, the phone calls to make, the emails to send, and the documents to read—it all seemed to blur. She didn't have the luxury of having time to reflect on her feelings. Work was her refuge and her fortress, a place where she could excel without a doubt.

But the confusion in her heart, the dissonance between her family's expectations and her own desires lingered like a shadow over her day. As she worked, Julie couldn't help but wonder if her pursuit of perfection had led her to a life where she was a master of her career, but a prisoner of her choices. Julie's life was becoming increasingly complex, and the path to understanding her own destiny seemed to be shrouded in uncertainty. Each day brought new challenges, both at work and in her personal life and Julie was at a crossroads, struggling with the decisions she had made and those she had not yet made.

Chapter 4: Home Sweet Home!

Julie's workday had finally come to an end, and the thought of going home to see Bagel filled her with joy and excitement. For her, the best part of every day was when she walked through the door of her house and her 11-year-old feline best friend greeted her. Julie loved Bagel more than she could express, more than she could ever love anyone else. To her, Bagel was her true soulmate, a source of unwavering affection and comfort that transcended any human relationship.

Despite living only, a 5-minute walk from her workplace, Julie chose to drive, because her position on the corporate ladder required a certain level of decorum and she couldn't afford to be seen arriving at the office on foot or by bike. It was a choice dictated by the expectations of her powerful career.

As she drove her luxurious green SUV through the picturesque streets of her town, "Anacaona," the traffic had unfortunately become an unpleasant companion. The minutes seemed like hours, and the desire to get home and reunite with Bagel, her beloved cat, was overwhelming.

Julie didn't think of freshly baked bread when she thought of home. No. It was the scent of her feline companion, Bagel, that Julie longed to breathe. The anticipation of this simple but profound pleasure was the driving force behind her daily commute home.

Finally, she arrived at her luxurious building and parked on level B3 and took the elevator to the 16th floor. The day seemed to be less heavy as she approached the door of her penthouse. With each step, she could feel the stress and commotion of the day melting away, a little at least. Her home was her sanctuary and Bagel was her comfort.

When she opened the door and entered, she found that throaty meow that melted her heart and that soft, hairy presence that rubbed against her leg. Julie's heart expanded and filled with love as she bent down to pick up her loyal friend, her son. Bagel's purr was like a relaxing spa, and it was at this moment, surrounded by her cat's unconditional love, that Julie found the peace she so desperately needed throughout the day.

Chapter 5: Love

Julie grabbed Bagel in her arms and talked nonsense to him in the most shrill, ridiculous voice she could find. Her relationship with Bagel was something truly extraordinary. She had rescued him from the unforgiving streets during one of her business trips to Paraguay. From the moment she saw him, she was totally in love. He was a small ball of hair, gray and white, with the most beautiful green eyes Julie had ever seen. His fur was the perfect length, and he was only a few weeks old. He was so tiny that he fit in the palm of her hands.

Julie knew she had to take him home with her. She couldn't bear to leave him behind. From that day on, Bagel had become the center of her world. He wasn't just a pet; he was her son, her family, and her best friend and confidant. She whispered her love to him in the sweetest tones, and Bagel answered with soft purrs, his way of reciprocating Julie's affection.

Julie was 38 years old and had no human children. The topic often circulated in not-so-low-key voices at her workplace, and Julie was well aware of the gossip. She knew that she was approaching the age where she needed to make life-changing decisions. Perhaps she was already past that age, but uncertainty filled her thoughts.

People expected her to marry Sam and hopefully have children before she was 40. It was an implicit rule in her family and social circle, a timeline etched in tradition and expectations. The pressures of this impending deadline weighed on Julie, despite her affection for Sam.

Julie understood the situation and the social norms she had to adhere to very well, but a part of her was cherishing a secret dream. It was the dream of growing old surrounded by cats, companions that would provide her with unconditional love and comfort throughout her life. Becoming the "crazy cat lady" certainly had its own charm. In that dream, it would be just her and her feline companions, living life on her own terms, divorced from the judgments and expectations of others.

As Julie continued to whisper sweet things to Bagel, she couldn't help but contemplate the paths ahead, each stacked with its own challenges and choices. Her life was becoming increasingly complex, and the decisions she would make over the next few years would shape her future in a way she could barely comprehend.

Chapter 6: Dissatisfaction

Julie tried to quietly enter the semi-dark bedroom, where Sam lay on the bed with his face lit up, engrossed in videos of beauty pageants playing on his electronic tablet. Sam and Julie watched these pageants together from time to time, but Julie couldn't shake the nagging question lingering in her mind. She wondered why Sam was so obsessed with beauty pageants. That latent question made her question the depth of Sam's preferences. Was it that he liked to see beautiful girls in bikinis, or was it something else entirely?

Despite knowing that Sam loved her, she couldn't help but wonder if he was still attracted to her. The spark they once felt in their relationship seemed to have dimmed over the years. The romance and passion she once felt with him now left room for doubt, and she could not pinpoint what had changed.

Strangely, Julie felt chained to Sam, as if she were a willing prisoner of her own life. As an efficient superhuman, Julie couldn't afford to let her doubts and insecurities lay bare. She had to maintain the façade of a perfect life, even when it was the opposite. From an outsider's perspective, her life was the stuff of dreams.

She was really wealthy and lived in a beautiful penthouse with a stunning view, right in front of Marina Willows Park. She had a luxury car, had the latest electronics, and enjoyed the fastest internet. She had a partner who, by society's standards, was perfect. Her life was one that many would envy, but for some reason, Julie couldn't find happiness in it.

Stress clung to her like a shadow, and the weight of her endless responsibilities fell on her like a bunch of rocks. Tiredness overwhelmed her for days and anxiety was her constant companion. The relentless demands of her life left her with little time for herself, and she couldn't escape the feeling that she really didn't deserve the life she was living.

Julie was pondering the question that had been gnawing at her for so long: What did she really want in life? As she stood in the bedroom, watching Sam watch the pageants, she couldn't deny the growing sense of discontent that had been taking root in her heart. The perfect façade of her life was crumbling, and she was now faced with the daunting challenge of confronting her own desires and searching for a way to find genuine happiness and fulfillment.

Chapter 7: Insomnia

Julie and Sam chatted about their respective workdays, as they usually did every night, exchanging the usual anecdotes that peppered their lives. It was a regular routine that marked the end of their days, offering them the appearance of a real connection amid their increasingly obvious problems.

As they settled into bed, the dim moonlight cast an atmosphere of peace over the room. With each passing minute, it was getting closer to bedtime. Julie closed her eyes, and like a clock with new batteries, a storm of thoughts and worries descended upon her.

Her upcoming wedding, the incessant list of goals for her possible promotion in the agency, and the complexities of managing the demanding Latin American account were seeping into her mind. She could not escape the relentless pressure of these responsibilities, even in her most vulnerable moments.

And then, her thoughts turned to Bagel, her beloved cat. His teeth were slowly rotting, a sign of his advanced age and the poor quality of cat foods, even those expensive ones Julie bought for him, as the vet had explained to her. Julie couldn't help but feel a deep sadness at the thought of this. Bagel was more than a pet; He was family and watching him get old was a heartbreaking experience.

But her worries did not end there. Maple, her lifelong friend and twin soul, had been acting strangely lately. Julie had noticed some signs of mania in her dearest friend. It was a troubling thing, and it weighed heavily on Julie's mind. Maple's well-being was very important to Julie.

Maple had always been like a sister to Julie, and their bond was unbreakable. They had known each other for as long as they could remember, and the thought of Maple struggling with her mental health was a heavy burden for Julie.

Beyond Maple, there was her younger brother, Michael. He was still a teenager and lived with their parents, Dinorah and Barry. Julie couldn't escape the worry that had gripped her heart. Michael was hanging out with the wrong crowd, smoking and drinking alcohol, acting rebellious. Julie knew he was a good kid, and his sudden change in behavior was cause for concern. But he refused to talk to her, excluding her.

Julie felt like she had no time for anyone, but she carried the weight of the world's worries on her shoulders. Her life was a relentless juggling act, but she remained steadfast in her commitment to maintaining a sweet, friendly smile for everyone around her.

As she lay on the bed, her thoughts swirled in endless circles, sinking her deeper into the web of her worries. She opened her eyes, the shadows in her room casting a silent reminder that this would be another sleepless night, another night where anxiety would accompany her in the dark.

Chapter 8: Midnight

Julie's eyes opened wide in the stillness of midnight, and the desire to work overcame her. She slid carefully out of bed, making sure not to disturb Sam, who lay fast asleep, snoring faintly. This, unfortunately, had become a habitual routine, a secret escape from the chaos of her life.

She made her way to the office on the second floor of the penthouse; it was like a sanctuary where she could focus and find peace amid the demands of her busy days. But tonight was something different. Julie needed a moment for herself. She sat down at her desk and indulged in a quick glance at her social media accounts.

When she grabbed her phone, the cobweb-like cracks in the screen caught her attention. She knew she had to call the phone company to get a replacement for the device. Her pricy plan made it easy, and her warranty was top-notch. She made a mental note to address it in the morning.

Julie's social media timeline was a mix of cute animal videos, news updates, and a few self-motivating posts. However, one video in particular stopped her in her tracks. Maple had uploaded it. She was in "Cuervo Hills", a part of Marina Willows Park known for the crows that congregated there.

In the video, Maple spoke very passionately about the universe and its interconnectedness with all living things. Julie was glued to the screen; Maple's words, although strange, made a lot of sense. It was an interesting perspective, but there was an intensity to Maple's behavior that Julie found unusual and although she didn't know how to explain it, something in her eyes was different.

Maple had undoubtedly always been a free spirit, but this seemed to be something else. Her words sounded like the ramblings of someone who had crossed the limits into a deeper realm of thought. Julie was concerned, as this was not the first video of this nature that Maple had posted on her social media. Maple wanted to be an online influencer.

As Julie continued to watch, concern was drawn on her face. She needed to talk to someone about Maple's mental health, and her mother, Dinorah, a licensed psychologist and therapist, was the first person that came to mind. Dinorah would certainly know how to approach the situation and offer her guidance.

Julie couldn't help but feel responsibility for her dear friend. As she contemplated her next steps, the complexities of her life continued to unfold, and Maple's mental well-being became another challenge Julie would have to deal with.

Chapter 9: Bagel

Julie closed her social media apps and left her office. She found Bagel napping serenely on the couch, watching him sleep gave her peace. Bagel was her comfort, her confidant, and her faithful companion in moments of anxiety. Julie had a bad tendency to wake him up at such times, seeking comfort in his presence.

Bagel's bad breath was a nagging reminder that she needed to address some of her concerns at the next vet appointment. His health was a top priority, and she couldn't let any problem, no matter how small, go unattended.

As she approached him, Bagel stretched his body and opened his eyes. He let out a soft, sleepy meow, acknowledging Julie's presence. She gently lifted him and placed him on her lap, hoping to enjoy his warm, gentle company for a few minutes.

However, Bagel had other plans. After just three seconds on her lap, he decided that his sleep was much more appealing. He climbed down gracefully, and with a carefree demeanor he approached one of the many beds Julie had thoughtfully arranged for him throughout the penthouse. With a sigh of satisfaction, Bagel settled in for another round of sleep in total peace and comfort.

Julie watched him absorbedly for a moment, a small smile on her lips. Bagel's ability to be himself, to find joy and fulfillment in the simplest things, was a reminder for Julie that sometimes it was okay to allow yourself to find peace amid life's chaos, it was the anchor she needed as she prepared for the conversations and decisions that lay ahead.

Chapter 10: Inspiration

Julie settled on the couch with her laptop, determined to work on the Latin American account. She always arrived early, but the thought of work piling up made her uneasy. She couldn't afford to lose focus, and for that reason, she wouldn't wear her headphones while working. A sharp mind was a non-negotiable requirement, and mistakes were a luxury she could not afford.

Among the many things on her to-do list, there was one that stressed her out quite a bit: she had to come up with an idea to control the Latin American market. The team had scheduled a brainstorming session for the morning, and they were facing a challenge against time. Julie was far from motivated or inspired, and that was a problem she couldn't ignore.

She knew that the opportunity presented to her was too important to let slip through her fingers. As she sat with her laptop open, the cursor blinking on the screen, she could feel the weight of her expectations upon her.

Julie closed her eyes for a moment, took a deep breath, and made a promise to herself. The next day, she would arrive at the office earlier than usual. She hoped that a fresh start and a change in her surroundings would help her regain her motivation and inspiration. The idea of not taking advantage of this opportunity was not an option she could accept.

With that decision made, Julie concluded her work for the night. She closed her laptop and returned to the bedroom, finding Sam lost in a soft snore, blissfully unaware of her nightly efforts.

With a cautious and deliberate attempt, Julie climbed into bed. She wanted to be as light as a feather, careful not to disrupt Sam's sleep. As she settled in, she closed her eyes and tried to clear her mind, hoping that the weight of the day's responsibilities would ease and allow her to find rest.

Chapter 11: The Visit

As Julie slowly stepped into the realm of dreams, her thoughts calmed down and a deep sense of relaxation enveloped her. In this vulnerable state of mind, she awoke abruptly. Her eyes widened, and she gasped audibly, surprised by something she couldn't quite comprehend.

In front of her, at a safe distance, stood the image of an old woman. The figure bore a striking resemblance to her "Nana" Minerva, her sweet grandmother, who had passed away when Julie was just 11 years old. Her heart raced with every second that seemed to be eternal, as she dealt with the impossible presence of someone she had thought was long gone.

Julie's mind was wrestling with the possibility that her imagination was playing tricks on her. She felt a mix of emotions, including disbelief, wonder, and a sense of longing for the grandmother she had loved so much.

Interestingly, for some strange reason, she wasn't afraid. The mysterious figure, which resembled her Nana, exuded an aura of peace and familiarity. It was as if the presence had something important to say to her. Julie, her voice trembling, whispered, "Come closer. I'm not afraid of you."

Sam's snoring filled the room with a soft, rhythmic but steady sound, providing the only sign that she wasn't completely alone in this strange encounter. The figure, whether a spirit or a ghost, approached Julie. Their gazes met, and the apparition's warm, soft hands reached out to grasp Julie's. The touch of that being felt the same as that of her grandmother when she was still alive.

In this deep and mysterious moment, Julie felt her thoughts unravel in her mind. Something inside her told her that the encounter was about to end, that it was a fleeting visit. The vision, with a deep and enigmatic look, conveyed an unusual message to her: "Absolute power does exist."

And then, as suddenly as it had appeared, the being disappeared, leaving Julie in a state of bewildered wonder. She blinked in the dim light of the room, her heart pounding, trying to reconcile herself with what had just happened. Had it been a strange dream, a figment of her imagination, or a genuine encounter with something beyond her comprehension?

She still felt the warmth of the spirit's touch, or whatever it was, a sensation that lingered and left her amazed but perplexed. As Julie lay in bed, pondering the unexplainable, she couldn't help but wonder what kind of cosmic joke the universe was playing on her.

Chapter 12: The Shower

Julie's eyes darted to the clock; Disbelief was drawn on her face. How could she have fallen asleep? The incessant meows of Bagel, who was waiting for his portion of soft food in the morning, were an unpleasant reminder that she would be late for work. Yes or yes. She couldn't believe it. Julie had always been proud of her punctuality.

Without hesitation, she picked up her phone and dialed the office. Her voice conveyed a sense of urgency as she explained the unforeseen delay. She assured her colleagues that she would arrive later than usual and hung up, her mind racing to catch up on the sudden change in her meticulously planned morning routine.

Quickly, she went to the kitchen. Bagel kept meowing, and she knew she couldn't make him wait any longer. She grabbed a can of cat food and opened it clumsily. Then, she grabbed the dirty bowl from the floor, as she always made sure that Bagel's bowl was spotless. She poured him a portion mixed with a little water, for his teeth.

Julie, determined to keep her home tidy and clean, immediately placed the dirty bowl in the dishwasher. Her mother, Dinorah, had instilled in her the value of a clean house, a house that functioned, and that principle remained firmly in Julie's life.

Once her beloved cat's food was tended to, Julie turned her attention to her own morning routine. She knew there wasn't a lot of time available, but there was one thing she just couldn't skip: a shower.

In a hurried burst, she climbed into the shower, letting the nearly boiling water cascade down on her. For Julie, even a quick shower had its own standards, thanks to her unwavering dedication to maintaining a sense of order and personal hygiene.

The hurried morning was far from the routine she had meticulously designed for herself, and she felt a lingering sense of chaos. The morning's events were like a stark reminder that the unexpected surprises life had in store could throw even the most organized and punctual people off balance.

Chapter 13: Priorities

Julie ran to her car, her heart pounding a thousand miles an hour as she waited for the inevitable traffic ahead. She needed to make up for lost time and she put on one of her favorite stations, 90's classics, to start the day with a good face, despite everything. As she sped down the street, the radio distracted her mind a bit in the midst of her hurried journey.

Every second counted, and Julie drove like a crazy person, her impatience showing as she navigated through a sea of vehicles. Frustration boiled inside her when she encountered drivers who seemed oblivious to the concept of traffic etiquette. In her mind, she couldn't help but yell, "Get out of the way, you fine piece of idiot!" She wouldn't actually yell, but she really wanted to.

But beneath the surface of her racing thoughts, there was one truly lingering. She could not get the vision of that being who had visited her during the night out of her head. It had felt so real, that figure that looked so much like her grandmother. Was it really her beloved Nana Minerva, or just a random spirit? she needed to stay grounded and focus on the challenges of the day, which were many and on top of it all, she knew she was going to be late.

"Absolute power does exist," it echoed in Julie's thoughts, but logic and common sense reminded her that the strange encounter was most likely just a figment of her imagination and her weariness. She needed to focus on the real-world problems at hand.

Julie arrived at the office safely, her heart still racing from the hectic morning. For a brief moment she thought if perhaps it would have been better to walk, or run, but she was already there, which was the important thing. She ran to the elevator, which was about to close. The person inside pressed the "Open Doors" button, which allowed her to slide inside. But when the doors closed, she couldn't believe her eyes. It was her mother, Dinorah.

Julie's confusion grew as the elevator began to ascend and she found her voice to ask, "Mom, what are you doing here?" Dinorah's face had a grave and worried expression as she tried to find the words to say what she had to say. "Julie! Why didn't you answer the phone? I've been trying to communicate with you non-stop. Your dad, Barry, is in the intensive care unit in the hospital. He had a heart attack. He is stable, but his condition is delicate. We don't know if he will survive."

The news hit Julie like a boxer in search of an Olympic medal. Her heart raced, and her mind went into shock. She had to make a split-second decision. Work or family? It wasn't even a question. Julie made up her mind in an instant, left the office behind and went to the hospital with her mother. The world, as she knew it, had changed in an instant, and her father's well-being now took precedence over everything else.

Chapter 14: I Can't Lose Him

As Julie drove unhinged to the hospital, her thoughts were filled with the enigmatic message from the spirit that seemed to be her grandmother: "Absolute power does exist." What did it mean, and why had she received this strange message? Julie couldn't help but wonder if it was something about a dictatorship or something like that. Absolute power, for some strange reason, sounded somewhat terrifying.

However, the reality of the situation before her forced her to keep her feet on the ground again. The message, while more than a figment of her imagination, did not offer an immediate solution to the crisis her father, Barry, was experiencing. At this terrible time, Julie couldn't even imagine how she could have control over the situation. There was no magic power that could improve her father's condition.

Questions and mysteries persisted, but Julie could not afford to be consumed by them. Her mother, Dinorah, needed her. There was no time to indulge in reflecting on ethereal messages.

When they arrived at the hospital, Dinorah held Julie's hands. Anguish etched on her face as she tried to calm down. Her voice trembled as she spoke the words that weighed heavily on her heart. "I can't lose him. He is my rock."

Julie, despite the confusion that dominated her interior, found a semblance of strength. She grabbed her mother's hands and looked into her eyes. "Dad is going to be fine, mom. I promise. Whatever happens, we will face it together."

At that moment, the questions that had arisen in her mind seemed irrelevant. The real power that mattered now was the strength of their bond and the determination to support each other in the face of the uncertainty that lay ahead.

Chapter 15: Sigh

Julie and Dinorah, heart-heavy with concern, sought out the nurse and asked her about Barry's condition. The nurse's words were like a balm to their anxious souls. "He's going to make it," she said with a reassuring smile. "He's awake and you can see him in a few minutes."

Both Julie and Dinorah sighed with deep relief, their faces lit up with the news. Their beloved Barry was going to pull through. The weight of uncertainty that had hung over them since the morning was dissipating, and a renewed sense of hope filled their hearts.

Before Julie went to see her father, she understood that it was essential to send an email to her office, explaining the circumstances and why she couldn't be there. Family had always been Julie's top priority, even before the prospect of the coveted Latin American account. She was determined to support her family during this difficult time.

She reached for her phone in her purse, but when her fingers touched the device, the sad reality slapped her in the face. She had forgotten to charge her phone. The screen was black and cracked, a visual reminder of an unfortunate oversight. Frustration and despair welled up incessantly within her.

Julie's thoughts raced as she grappled with the dilemma. She had always been punctual, an exemplary worker who gave her all in her work. Her dedication deserved recognition, but at this crucial time, her family needed her by their side. Work, important as it was, had to take a back seat to the urgent matters of life.

As Julie contemplated her next steps, the nurse called out to them, informing them that they could finally see Barry. There was no longer any room for hesitation or worry about her phone. Julie's priority was clear, and she followed the nurse along with Dinorah to the room where her father, her rock, was waiting.

Chapter 16: Have You Forgot About Your Father?

Barry Goldbucket was the embodiment of the kind of man Julie had always admired. He was not only an exceptional father, but also a devoted husband and a wise professional. Recently retired from his job as an accountant, he was reflecting on how to spend his newfound free time. Despite being aware that his heart wasn't quite ready for such an endeavor, he focused on his health and bought himself an elliptical to help him in his effort to lose a little belly.

When Julie and Dinorah entered the hospital room, Barry's eyes filled with gratitude and happiness at the sight of his family. Julie's brother Michael was still in school and her younger sister, Sophie, was somewhere in the world on vacation with her boyfriend of the moment.

However, there was something important that Barry felt compelled to share with his daughter, Julie. He knew that his wife, Dinorah, might consider it exaggerated, so he asked, "Dinorah, would you mind if I have a moment alone with Julie?" Confusion crept across Dinorah's face, but she reluctantly agreed and left the room.

Alone with Julie, Barry began, "Hey, my beautiful little girl, I haven't seen you in weeks. Have you forgotten about your father? A lone tear ran down Julie's cheek and she replied, "Dad, I'm sorry, really, you know how much I love you. It's work that has had me overwhelmed, but I'm sorry, I know it's not an excuse."

Barry reassured her: "It's okay, honey. I need to tell you something, but I'm afraid your mother will think I've lost my mind.

Julie was eager to hear what her father had to say and encouraged him: "What's up, Dad?"

Barry took a deep breath and shared his extraordinary experience. "Julie, I know that what I am going to tell you will seem crazy, if I had not experienced it in the flesh, I myself would doubt it, but, I have just visited another realm, another world, another dimension, I don't know. The fact is, believe it or not, I saw your grandmother Minerva. She sent you a message, told me to tell you that all the answers you're looking for lie in nature."

Julie listened intently as her father continued to describe the extraordinary world he had been in. "Julie, I followed the light. It was absolutely stunning. I saw a variety of colors that I didn't even know existed, I saw loved ones along my path, I heard beautiful melodies and for a few moments I felt immense clarity, and I understood everything, life, death, time, space, everything. Mom also told me that it was not my time yet, that I should go back. I wanted to stay with her, but I thought of Dinorah. I thought of you. I thought of Sophie and Michael."

Barry was worried that Dinorah wouldn't understand his experience, so he begged Julie to keep it a secret between the two of them. Julie, despite her initial confusion, agreed to fulfill her father's wish and confided to him, "Dad, I believe you and... you won't believe it, but I also saw Nana Minerva. She came to visit me last night; I saw her and felt her warmth...

The nurse, who entered the room together with Dinorah, interrupted their conversation and with an indifferent voice informed them, "I'm sorry, but the visiting time is over. Your dad needs to rest." Dinorah leaned over to give her husband a sweet little kiss on the forehead, and she and Julie reluctantly left the room, a little calmer.

Chapter 17: I'll Never Be Ready

When Julie and Dinorah left the hospital room, Julie expressed her concern and offered her help to Dinorah. "Let me know if you or Dad need anything. I have to rush to work; I'll be super late, and I've got a lot of work. I love you." She gave her mother a big hug and then ran to her car.

Dinorah, who had accompanied Julie to the hospital in Julie's car, shouted, "Julie, wait. My car is in your office.

Julie sighed and replied, "I'm sorry, Mom, run and I'll take you." They hurriedly got into Julie's car, and while they were inside, Dinorah asked about her previous conversation with Barry. "Tell me something, honey. What did your dad say to you?"

Julie had to think on the fly and quickly made up a little white lie. She replied, "Dad just wanted to let me know that he loved me and wanted me to take care of you, Sophie, and Michael if anything ever happened to him."

Dinorah's eyes filled with tears, and she whispered, "I hope Barry never abandons us. I'm just not ready. I never will be ready."

Julie got closer to comfort her mother. "Mom, we have to be prepared for that possibility, but don't worry for now. Dad is fine."

As they parked in Julie's office building, Julie gave her mother a big hug and a kiss on the cheek before rushing to her office. Her assistant, Benjie, greeted her with a stack of documents to sign and briefed her on the day's meetings. Fortunately, the morning had been relatively quiet, and Julie's absence had not caused major disruptions.

The day ahead was certainly challenging for Julie, with an overwhelming workload and many thoughts weighing on her mind.

Balancing the well-being of her family and the demands of her stressful career was no easy task, but Julie always found a way to navigate the complex terrain of her life with grace and determination.

Chapter 18: Remember Rule #1

While Julie sat in her office, drowning in a sea of paperwork and tasks, Benjie knocked on the door and let himself in. He then said, Guess what! I heard somewhere that they are going to fire the old hag from Human Resources. Julie couldn't stand her, but at that moment she didn't care about the gossip, the weight of her responsibilities weighing on her shoulders. The feeling of being overwhelmed led her to seek comfort in the one person who always seemed to provide it: her best friend, Maple.

Maple answered the phone, and her unusually cheerful tone caught Julie's attention. Worried, Julie asked, "Maple, are you okay? I'm really worried about you."

Maple's response, however, only added to Julie's confusion. "I feel better than ever, Julie. Remember rule number one and most of all remember that... West is Best," she replied.

Julie couldn't comprehend anything. The sudden change in her friend's behavior was worrying, no doubt, but she continued with her own explanation of what was happening to her. "Hey, I'm super overwhelmed with work today. I'm going to be a little late for girls' night, but I can't wait to see you and chill a bit. I have so many things to tell you."

Maple, who still radiated an unusual level of joy, reminded Julie again. "Remember rule number one."

Julie had forgotten her rule and asked for a reminder. Maple's answer was simple but enigmatic: "Rule number one is that you have to have fun."

Julie's face was a mixture of confusion and curiosity as she replied, "Ok, alright. I will try to remember that. I have to go now. I love you too much, friend. Stay out of trouble."

With some work set aside to finish at home in the evening, Julie rushed to complete the remaining tasks for the day and then headed home to prepare for girls' night.

Upon her arrival, her faithful companion, Bagel, who was waiting for her by the door, greeted her with his typical hoarse meows. Julie showered him with affection, and after a few kisses and hugs, she ran to the bathroom for a quick shower.

As the nearly boiling water from the shower fell on her body, Julie's mind couldn't help but go back to the enigmatic messages she had recently received. Her grandmother, Minerva, had left her the strange message that "Absolute power does exist" and her father told her that she had sent her another message, that "all the answers lie in nature". These messages continued to baffle Julie.

Adding to the intrigue was Maple's unusual message: "Rule number one is that you have to have fun." Julie's thoughts swirled in circles as she contemplated the meaning behind these unusual statements. She reminded herself that she had little time for supernatural or mystical things and needed to keep her focus on what really mattered at the time; her father's health, her friend's mental health, her cat's dental health, the Latin American account and the possible promotion to partner, the wedding, everything.

She lathered her skin with the luxurious soap she had grown accustomed to and allowed her worries and responsibilities to melt away, if only for a fleeting moment of peace. Girls' night was on the horizon, and it was the perfect opportunity for Julie to relax, confide in her best friend, and maybe find some answers in the company of Maple, who knew her better than anyone else.

Chapter 19: Girls' Night

After her hot shower, Julie stepped into her spacious dressing room to select comfortable, casual clothes and shoes for the girls' night with Maple. It was a time to kick back, relax on the couch, spend some time with Pancake, Maple's dog and catch up on their favorite show "Race for Fashion", enjoy some Carmenere wine and share life's little moments. Before leaving her penthouse, she took a moment to shower Bagel, her beloved cat, with affection, reminding him of all her love.

Julie checked that she had everything she needed before she closed the door: her wallet, her phone, and her keys. She then took the elevator to parking lot B3 and ran to her car, ready for the short drive to Maple's house. Julie didn't like to be late, even to girls' night.

Upon arriving at Maple's building, Julie buzzed intercom number 228. Maple answered, "Julie, you're finally here! Come on in" and let her in. Upon entering the building's lobby, Julie knew that Maple's apartment was only on the second floor, so she opted for the stairs. Maple waited at the top of the stairs and her eyes shone with unusual happiness. She hugged Julie and expressed her deep affection and the importance of their friendship. Maple's words touched Julie, but she also felt worried, feeling that something might be wrong with her friend's mental state.

Together, they walked to Maple's apartment. Pancake, Maple's dog, began to howl with excitement at the sight of Julie. Pancake adored her. When Julie entered the apartment, she quickly realized that she had forgotten the wine. She mentioned it to Maple, who replied with an enigmatic twinkle in her eye.

"Julie, life is eternal, love is infinite, happiness is a choice," Maple declared. She then suggested that they visit the liquor store downstairs to buy a bottle of wine. Julie was even more perplexed by Maple's strange words and responded with her trademark phrase, "I don't know, Maple, I don't know."

Maple, still radiating an unusual sense of satisfaction, reassured her: "Come on, come on."

As they prepared to go to the liquor store, Julie wondered to herself about the strange transformation she was witnessing in her best friend and the enigmatic messages that seemed to surround her life lately.

Chapter 20: I'm So Confused

At the liquor store, Julie and Maple made their way to the international wine section, where they selected a bottle of Chilean Carmenere, Julie's favorite wine. After Julie paid for the wine, they returned to Maple's apartment. Before enjoying their favorite show, "Race for Fashion," a show that followed designers from around the world as they competed to create garments for live runway shows against the clock, they enjoyed a variety of plant-based snacks that Maple had prepared for girls' night. Julie opened the bottle of Carmenere, and they settled into Maple's gray sectional couch.

Before hitting play on the remote, Maple turned to Julie and asked her how things were going with her work and life, asked her about her relationship with Sam and about the health of her cat, Bagel. Julie felt that Maple's unusual behavior was an indication of something more serious.

Julie let out a sigh and shared her thoughts. "Honestly, it's a lot, Maple. I'm really overwhelmed with work, especially with the Latin American account. I worry about the possibility of eventually becoming a partner, although it is something I want with all my might. I am worried about the additional workload that comes with the position. As for Sam, things are fine, I guess. I love him, I have no doubt about that, but I'm not sure if I'm still in love with him and I have a lot of doubts about whether he feels the same way. I don't even know if he's still attracted to me. Honestly, I don't know. And then there's Bagel, who's as sweet as ever, but his teeth are rotting and his breath stinks."

As Julie took a sip of wine, she contemplated the strange encounter that had recently occurred. "Maple, something really weird happened to me," she said. "And I forgot to tell you: my father had a heart attack."

Maple automatically expressed concern and asked about Barry's condition. Julie assured her that her father was okay and then said, "Maple, I'm so confused."

Maple suggested that they asked her divination deck for answers. Julie was hesitant, but the prospect of looking to the divination cards for guidance seemed appropriate at this time, considering the mysterious events of her life. Honestly, curiosity took over her being, which led her to see what the cards could reveal, so she accepted Maple's proposal.

Chapter 21: The Wisdom of the Cards

Maple studied the cards in front of her, her eyes focused on the intricate symbols and meticulous imagery they contained. The "Box of Shadows", with its dark and enigmatic illustration of an antique wooden box wrapped in ropes; represented the problem. It was as if the universe recognized the hidden and confusing aspects of Julie's life that had been troubling her.

Maple began by saying, "The 'Box of Shadows' tells us that the problems you face, Julie, are hiding in the dark." "You may struggle with something that isn't immediately apparent, or maybe you've kept certain emotions or thoughts hidden from yourself or others."

Julie couldn't help but nod with her head. The card's depiction seemed to resonate with the mysteries surrounding her recent experiences.

Maple moved on to the second card, the "Forest of Contemplation." This card represented the solution, and its image illustrated a lush forest, full of wildflowers and animals that radiated peace. It was strange, but it seemed that the cards offered Julie a path to find the answers she was looking for.

"The 'Forest of Contemplation' suggests that you should take some time for introspection," Maple explained. "Find a quiet space, like the forest in the card, a place where you can reflect on your thoughts and feelings. It is within yourself that you will discover the solutions you are looking for. You live across the street from Marina Willows, you should take a walk and disconnect from it all."

Julie pondered the meaning of this card. The idea of finding herself and seeking clarity through introspection resonated with her, given the challenges she faced.

Finally, Maple pulled out the card: "The Mirrored Lake." This card represented the future. The illustration showed a chromed lake that reflected the beauty of the forest and the mountains in the background. It seemed to convey a sense of clarity and serenity that seduced Julie.

Maple revealed, "The Mirrored Lake suggests that by finding that inner clarity in the 'Forest of Contemplation,' you will see a clear reflection of your future. It can be a time of peace, understanding, and a deeper connection with your own inner self."

Julie found comfort in the message of this card. It seemed to offer hope that, through introspection and self-discovery, she could find the way to a more harmonious future.

The best friends shared a moment of reflection, contemplating the messages on the divination cards that Maple had created. Julie couldn't help but feel that, in this sacred practice for many, she had found a ray of light that could guide her out of the shadows of uncertainty and into a brighter future.

They put the cards aside, and Maple pressed the play button on her remote. "Race for Fashion" had begun, Julie's mind filled with thoughts about her recent experiences, the mysterious spirit that resembled her grandmother Minerva, and the profound messages she had obtained from the divination cards. Even though the answers remained hidden, Julie felt capable of uncovering them, even if she had to embark on a journey within herself.

Chapter 22: West is Best

As they watched the latest episode of "Race for Fashion" and host "Gleeter" thanked sponsors, Julie's mind continued to wander, lost in a maze of thoughts and doubts. She couldn't escape the mystique of the revelations of Maple's cards or the messages she had received from the spirit of her Nana Minerva, or whoever it was. The idea of "all the answers lie in nature" seemed to align with the cards. She wondered if there was a deeper connection between divination and the message of this mysterious being.

Then there was the strange phrase that ghost had revealed to her: "Absolute power does exist." Perhaps the strangest thing was the emphasis on "does". It wasn't simply that absolute power existed, it was a confirmation that yes, absolute power was real. The mystery hung in the air like an unsolved enigma. Did it have anything to do with the "Mirrored Lake" card? Julie questioned the validity of these experiences. She debated whether they were real or mere figments of her imagination. After all, Maple had created those cards herself, and Maple was somewhat... Unconventional.

Julie once again noticed Maple's unusual behavior, which interrupted her internal debate. Her best friend had always been an eccentric, a self-proclaimed hippie. But tonight, Maple seemed disconnected from reality. Julie couldn't shake her growing concern for Maple's mental well-being.

When Maple's roommate Ria came out of her room bringing with her an empty plate of her typical noodle soup, Julie discreetly called her and expressed her concerns regarding Maple. She asked her to keep an eye on her and let her know if anything seemed wrong. Ria, with her calm nature, agreed to take care of her friend and notify Julie if she noticed anything concerning.

When Maple returned from the bathroom, Julie decided it was time to leave. She expressed her gratitude for the pleasant evening, the delicious vegan snacks, and the reading of the cards. She hugged Maple tightly and thanked her for her hospitality, promising to call her the next day. Before leaving, Maple reminded her again... West is Best!

Julie left Maple's apartment and drove home, feeling a mix of emotions: gratitude for her incredible friendship with Maple, obviously concern for her best friend's well-being, and a nagging sense of doubt regarding the supernatural experiences that had unfolded around her. She could not shake the meaning of "West is best" from her mind. It wasn't the first time Maple had said this. When she arrived at her house, Bagel, her faithful cat, greeted her joyfully, while he rubbed against her legs. Julie filled Bagel with affection, telling him how handsome and adorable he was, but she couldn't shake the uncertainty that had taken over her mind.

Chapter 23: Marina Willows

Julie entered her bedroom, the moon casting a soft bluish glow on the walls. Sam was still fast asleep, wrapped up in his own dreams, softly snoring. She couldn't stop thinking about the messages she'd received, Maple's cards, and her vivid experiences the other night. The idea of finding answers in nature tugged at her conscience.

Julie couldn't resist the pull any longer. She would go to Marina Willows Park in the morning, where She could find solace and clarity amidst the beauty of the park. Marina Willows had always been a special place for her, a place where she could escape the pressures of her busy life and let her thoughts wander, at least for a moment. Plus, the direct view of the park from her penthouse only made her love it more.

She put on her pajamas, with Bagel's beautiful face, a gift that Maple had given her a few Christmases ago. Julie went to the kitchen, opened the fridge, took a few oranges out of the fruit drawer and made herself a glass of freshly squeezed orange juice, after drinking her juice she went to the room trying not to make too much noise, she carefully got into bed next to Sam, cautious not to disturb his sleep. In the silence of the room, she prayed to the universe, expressing her need for help and clarity, hoping that someone or something might be listening to her. However, the room remained still, and no voice answered.

She closed her eyes again, hoping for a quiet night. Incredibly, it was a truly restful sleep, with no dreams to overwhelm her thoughts, like a screen turned off. When the clock struck 7:22 a.m., Julie woke up, ready for a new day, feeling refreshed and eager to embark on her quest for clarity at Marina Willows.

Sam had already gotten up and had attended to Bagel, who received her with a mixture of affection and a lot of hunger since he was always hungry... Always. After a quick shower and getting dressed, Julie knew she had a mission. She grabbed a bag of peanuts to feed the park squirrels, her gym water bottle to stay hydrated, and, of course, her latest-model Pineapple headphones. The park was her destination, and the whispers of nature beckoned her to find those answers she so desperately needed.

Julie's morning walk through Marina Willows was a relaxing experience. She lived right across from the park, and it had always been a special place for her, a place where she could clear her mind and find solace in the midst of the beauty of nature.

As she strolled, the ethereal songs of "Sky Water" played in her headphones, making the tranquility of the morning even more relaxing. Julie was walking through the Duck Lagoon, her steps led her to a bench, where she intended to sit to watch the ducks, geese, crows, seagulls and even blue herons that used to prowl the lagoon: on the bench there was a painted rock adorned with what appeared to be intricate alien symbols in shiny gold paint. On the back of the rock, were the numbers 10:25. Julie asked herself if it was one of Maple's artistic creations. The cryptic message no doubt intrigued her. Could it be possible that the symbols had some meaning relevant to her dilemmas? Julie asked herself. She picked up the rock and placed it in her bag. It was as if the universe had left her with a little mystery to solve.

Julie continued her walk through the park, passing through an area that Maple had affectionately nicknamed "the Serengeti" because of its resemblance to the African landscapes in the nature documentaries she used to watch with her father as a child. She stopped under a majestic oak tree with twisted branches, closed her eyes, and took a deep breath, enjoying the warm rays of the sun on her face. The phrase "Absolute power does exist" resonated in her thoughts. She contemplated its meaning: Did it signify her own inner strength and the potential she had as a strong, independent woman, or was it a message of even greater importance?

Lost in thought, Julie took off her headphones and immersed herself in the sounds of the park, hoping to find the answers she was looking for.

She looked at the spiky petaled purple flowers, the yellow and white daffodils, the pink aster flowers. Chubby fuzzy bees seemed to float above the beautiful flowers. Under an oak tree she saw an iridescent hummingbird, with violet, green, pink, and blue tones. The crows suddenly began to squawk in unison. Julie turned to look at them and it seemed that they wanted to tell her something.

Chapter 24: Clarity

Julie walked to an area of Marina Willows that people called "The Enchanted Forest" but that her friend Maple called "The Fairy Forest". The breathtaking beauty of that wooded area of the park captivated Julie as she went deeper. The towering trees created dappled shadows on the ground and the vibrant green, yellow, and orange leaves crunched in the gentle breeze. She found a place away from the crowd and sat down on a worn green wooden bench, surrounded by the sounds of nature. Birds sang their melodies, squirrels scampered in the distance, and a small babbling stream could be heard in the background.

Julie placed the peculiar rock she had found on the other bench beside her, and it shone in the sunlight. She stared at it, contemplating the meaning of the "alien" symbols and the numbers "10:25". It was a mystery she couldn't ignore.

Taking a deep breath, Julie closed her eyes and allowed her senses to absorb the beauty and tranquility of the "Fairy Forest." The whispers of the wind through the leaves of the trees seemed to speak to her, they seemed to tell her that in nature there was a greater connection to the universe and that maybe, just maybe, Maple's unorthodox wisdom had a kernel of truth.

She thought about that conversation with her father: how he had briefly traveled to another realm of existence and met his mother and Julie's grandmother, Minerva. Julie remembered the enigmatic phrase about absolute power, she thought of the box of shadows, of the mirrored lake, of the forest of contemplation, and of how Maple's words had offered her a glimmer of understanding in the face of the mysteries of existence.

Julie realized that Marina Willows, with its stunning natural beauty, was her mirrored lake. She looked at the rock again and suddenly it occurred to her that the numbers 10:25 could perhaps represent the time: that day, at 10:25am, she was there in the park, looking for answers in nature. It felt like a small revelation, a piece of a puzzle that was coming together.

Julie took a deep breath. She was open to the possibility that nature would not only have comfort for her anxiety but also answers to her questions. As she continued her walk, she felt an inexplicable connection to the world around her.

For the first time in a long time, Julie allowed herself to be fully present in the moment, let go of the weight of her responsibilities, and appreciate the perfect beauty of the natural world. It was as if the universe had offered her a memorandum that absolute power, whether as strength, clarity, or understanding, was not out of reach.

Julie would later share this revelation with Maple, but she still didn't feel ready to reveal some of her secrets. With each breath, Julie set out to explore the mysteries of life, the messages of the universe, and the power of the natural world. In this peaceful moment, in the midst of Marina Willows' beauty, Julie found the clarity and strength she had been looking for a long time. The future held challenges and opportunities, but at that moment, the only thing that seemed to matter was the fullness she felt amid nature.

Chapter 25: The Sea

Julie walked towards the ocean along the path and there was a small fawn eating from the grass of a meadow full of flowers of all colors, the grass was so tall that it blocked the view of the street that led to the beach.

Julie crossed the street, passed by the dog park and stared at them for a while. The joy of the dogs made her a little envious. Then she went down the wooden stairs to the rocky beach and stood there by the water's edge, gazing at the endless expanse of the ocean. The waves danced rhythmically, and their gentle crashes created a soothing music. The salty sea breeze carried with it a sense of freedom, a reminder that there was a vast world beyond her everyday life, full of opportunity, mysteries, and unexplored beauty.

As she looked at the pebbles beneath her feet, Julie couldn't help but think of the burdens she'd been carrying for so long. Each stone symbolized a doubt, a responsibility or a concern and weighed on her like a truck full of cement. She thought about what the universe had been trying to tell her through her father, through her grandmother, through Maple's mysticism, and through the beauty of Marina Willows and the majestic ocean.

With a newfound clarity, Julie decided that she needed to let go of some of those rocks to eliminate the burdens that no longer served her. It was a liberating thought, one that filled her with hope and a sense of lightness. As she watched the waves wash over the stones of the beach over and over again, she imagined that those worries went away with the waves and dissolved in the vastness of the ocean.

Julie couldn't help but feel a deep connection to nature that was intertwined with the human experience of that moment. Nature seemed to offer comfort, inspiration, and answers when sought, knowing that nature was indeed a source of wisdom and healing. Julie was grateful for the insights she had gained on this introspective walk.

Julie took a handful of those pebbles as a memo of this moment, a reminder that she could always return to Marina Willows, to the beach, to the river, to the lake, to find peace and release her burdens. As she picked up some stones and placed them in her bag, she felt lighter and more connected to the world around her. For now, she was still savoring the simple pleasures of the ocean and the tranquility of the moment.

As the sun dug below the horizon, casting vibrant hues of orange and pink in the sky, Julie took one last deep breath and began her journey back home, carrying with her the day's lessons, a few stones, and the promise of a brighter, more connected future.

Chapter 26: New Dawn

The next day at work, Julie woke up with a strange new sense of clarity and purpose. She felt lighter, as if someone had lifted a weight off her shoulders. The experience in the park had left an indelible mark on her and she had begun to accept the messages she had received from her father, her grandmother, Maple, and the mysterious universe itself.

She started her day as usual, taking great care of her routine. Julie was not one to neglect her appearance; She knew that looking good almost always made her feel more confident. As she got dressed, she reflected on the meaning of "Absolute power does exist." Those words were like a mantra in her mind, urging her to make the most of her inner strength and potential in every way.

Before leaving for work, she decided to call Maple, who had been acting mysteriously happy the night before. Julie felt it was time to talk about her concerns about her friend's mental well-being. She called her and suggested that they meet at "Hexabux" for coffee later that day.

After the call with Maple, Julie headed to her office, ready to tackle the day's work. She was surprised by her own enthusiasm, which had been rare lately. Perhaps the visit to the park had stirred something inside her, awakening her passion and motivation.

The day at the office passed curiously quickly and Julie's coworkers certainly noticed her energy and focus. Benjie even suggested that she not drink any more coffee. As the brainstorming session for the Latin American account approached, she felt an unusual emotion build up inside her. She felt she had the power to make a real impact, to use her position and influence to bring about positive change. The concept of "absolute power" took on a new meaning.

At the meeting, Julie presented her ideas confidently and eloquently. She felt a deep connection between her colleagues and the potential of the project. As the discussion flowed, her vision resonated with the team. For the first time in a long time, Julie felt the true power of her abilities. Apparently, Mr. Chespirito was quite impressed, and according to Woodfire's grinning face from his office, it seemed that there was a deal in the crosshairs.

As the workday ended, Julie's thoughts turned to her next coffee with Maple. She was eager to talk about the events of the past few days, to hear her friend's perspective on the messages and experiences she had lived. Julie couldn't help but think that maybe they were both on a similar journey of self-discovery.

She left the office and headed to Hexabux, where she saw Maple sitting at a corner table, engrossed in a notebook filled with colorful illustrations and doodles. Julie approached her friend with a warm smile, ready to have a conversation that might bring some clarity and understanding to her mysterious experiences.

As the two friends sipped their coffee, Julie realized that she didn't need to have all the answers at once; She could rely on the wisdom of her inner being, the strength of her relationships, and the power of the natural world around her. Julie decided to keep the visit of her Nana Minerva's ghost a secret. For Julie, this was meant to remain undisclosed, at least for now. She understood that Maple was going through a personal moment of confusion and apparently a mental health episode. Talking to her about ghosts didn't seem to be a good idea in her somewhat manic state.

Choosing to keep quiet about things at times when it wasn't convenient to talk about them was in some ways the beginning of a new chapter in her life, one full of potential for growth, self-discovery, and a deep connection to the world around her. She understood that existence was an ever-evolving adventure.

The sun was setting outside the window of the café, casting a golden glow on the faces of two friends who were experiencing something extraordinary simultaneously. When they went their respective ways, Julie kept repeating the mantra "Absolute power does exist" in her head.

Chapter 27: Answer the Phone!

Julie's heart raced with worry when her repeated calls to her father, Barry, went unanswered. Her conversation with her mother, Dinorah, had been brief, but the mention of her father playing dominoes in the park had triggered a sense of urgency in her. She couldn't shake the feeling that something bad might have happened.

She ran to the elevator, went down to the lobby, and exchanged hurried words with the janitor as she left the building. Marina Willows was just across the street, and she ran like a bullet, anxiety eating away at her at every turn.

As Julie made her way into the park, she surveyed the area, her eyes leaping from one group of people to another in search of her father's face. The late afternoon bathed the park in a warm, golden light, casting long shadows on the ground. The children who were playing on the swings began to leave, the couples that walked hand in hand started walking towards the exit of the park and the elderly residents who were enjoying the tranquility of the park and feeding the pigeons, began to collect their belongings. But Barry was nowhere to be found.

Julie continued her search, walking the park's winding paths, hoping to find a group of people playing dominoes somewhere. There was no one at the picnic tables. She asked some people he saw along the way if they had seen her father, but their answers were useless. Anxiety and worry took over her mind. Barry had recently had a heart attack, and she couldn't help but fear the worst.

As the minutes turned into what seemed like hours, Julie saw someone sitting on a bench in the distance where her father sometimes sat to feed the crows. Near the bench there was a really unusual tree, it looked like a person with their arms raised. Julie approached the bench with a heavy heart and a sinking feeling, hoping it was him and that he was okay, of course. There, right in front of her, a chunky, half-bald, white-haired man could be seen from behind. He was unmistakable; it was her father, Barry.

Relief came over Julie as she approached her father. The vibrant array of flowers surrounding the bench stole her attention for an instant, their colors matching the setting sun. Barry seemed lost in thought, the wrinkles on his face etched with a mixture of contemplation and contentment.

"Daddy," Julie said, her voice full of concern and relief. Barry looked up, and his eyes lit up at the sight of his daughter.

"Julie, my beautiful little girl," he said, grinning from ear to ear. "You found me!"

Julie couldn't hold back tears of relief. She hugged her father with all her might, feeling his presence and the unmistakable bond they shared. She asked, "Dad, why didn't you answer my calls? I was going crazy, thinking that something had happened to you."

Barry's gaze turned to the beautiful flowers for an instant and he tapped his hand three times on the space beside him on the bench. Julie took a seat, and her father spoke to her in a reassuring voice.

"I'm sorry I didn't answer, Julie. But honestly, I needed a moment, you know? Just being here and appreciating the beauty of life. Sitting with the flowers and letting the world stop for a moment. The heart attack gave me the clarity I needed; I have to make the most of the time I have left..."

Julie listened intently to her father's words, understanding that he needed that respite, that connection to the natural world around him. She realized that his recent experiences had given him a deeper appreciation of the subtleties of life and the importance of being present in the moment.

"I get it, Dad," Julie said with a smile. "Sometimes, we all need to step back and just be."

Barry nodded, his eyes shining with wisdom. "Exactly, my little girl. Life is a beautiful gift from the universe, and we must cherish it with every breath. I know your mind is always racing, but sometimes, the peace and answers we seek are right in front of us."

Julie and her father, Barry, shared a peaceful moment of understanding and connection. The worries of the day seemed to fade away, replaced by a deep sense of gratitude for the simplicity of life and the love they had for each other.

Julie understood that her father's message about being present matched her own recent experiences and the wisdom she had gained from her time alone at Marina Willows. It was a lesson she knew she could take with her, not only in her personal life, but also in her career. The power to make a difference lay not only in ambition, but in appreciating the beauty of the world around her.

At that moment, as the sun set on the horizon and the golden glow of twilight bathed the park, Julie and Barry went home.

Chapter 28: The Big Day

Julie had been waiting for this day for months with a strange mixture of excitement and anxiety. Today was her great opportunity to get that promotion that would finally make her a partner of the prestigious agency where she worked, "Irguitzu Marketing Ltd.", It was the culmination of years of hard work, dedication and perseverance. The presentations for the Latin American account had been a success, and it was time for her to reap the rewards.

As she prepared for her day at the office, Julie felt a nervous energy coursing through her body. She felt the weight of responsibility that came with being a partner in a prestigious marketing agency. The stakes were high, and she had worked tirelessly to make sure she was prepared for this moment.

With her well-prepared presentation in hand, Julie headed to the office early, determined to give it her all. She knew she had to impress Woodfire, the senior partners, and especially Mr. Chespirito, during the meeting. The outcome of this meeting would shape her future, and she was determined to make the most of this opportunity.

As she entered the meeting room together with her assistant, Benjie, the stern faces of the senior partners greeted her. The tension in the room was palpable, but Julie kept her composure. She had rehearsed her presentation countless times and was confident in her abilities.

Julie began her presentation with confidence and conviction. She outlined the details of the account for the Latin American market, the potential for growth, and the strategic advantages it would bring to both the agency and the brand. She spoke eloquently, weaving together her years of experience and her unwavering dedication to the firm.

As the presentation progressed, Julie could see the senior partners becoming more interested and attentive. Their initial skepticism seemed to fade as they recognized the importance of the opportunity. She could feel that she was making a powerful impression.

After what seemed like an eternity, Julie concluded her presentation. Mr. Chespirito left the room in a moment of silence and went to Woodfire's office with him. The senior partners exchanged glances and then Mr. Woodfire, finally returned to the meeting room.

"Julie, your performance was really outstanding," he said, and his serious expression softened into a smile. "You've shown us that you have the vision, dedication and drive to become a partner in this agency."

Julie felt her heart swell with pride and relief. She had succeeded. She had impressed Woodfire, the main partners and Chespirito. Promotion was within her reach. The weight of the moment lightened, and Julie knew her life was about to change.

The other main partners also expressed their approval, including Joan, confirming Julie's promotion to partner. It was a moment of triumph, the culmination of years of hard work and determination.

When Julie left the meeting room, she thought about all the sacrifices she had made to get to that moment. She had faced many challenges, put aside her personal life, and worked tirelessly to achieve those goals. But she had also learned valuable lessons along the way.

That chapter of her life had turned a new page. Julie was on the path to a brilliant career and a future full of possibilities. She would carry with her the wisdom she had gained from her experiences, not only in her career, but in all aspects of her life. Julie looked forward to the challenges and opportunities that lay ahead. She had proven that she had what it took to succeed.

Chapter 29: Don't Get Excited Too Quickly

Julie was on top of the world after getting her promotion to partner at the marketing agency. It was a defining moment in her career, and she couldn't have been happier. The next few days at the company were filled with celebrations, recognition from her colleagues, and even a congratulatory note from CEO Mr. Woodfire that had made her blush.

However, the next day, as she sat at her desk, her phone rang, displaying the name "Thomas Woodfire" on the screen. Her heart raced as she answered the call. "Hello, eh, Mr. Woodfire," she greeted him with a mixture of excitement and nervousness.

But what she heard next shattered her world. The voice on the other end of the line did not bring good news. Mr. Woodfire's tone, on the other hand, was serious and unforgiving.

"Miss Goldbucket," he began, "I'm afraid we must let you go."

Stunned, Julie felt her heart sink, struggling to find the words to answer. She was shaking nervously and could barely find the words to answer. "Let me go?" she finally stammered. "What do you mean, Mr. Woodfire?"

Mr. Woodfire's response was devastating. "We have discovered that your master's degree in "International Marketing" is nothing more than a lie, a worthless piece of paper. You have presented false credentials to the company, which is a serious breach of trust."

Julie felt the color slip from her face as the weight of Woodfire's words settled. She was aware of the rumors circulating about her false qualifications, but she believed it was obvious that the rumors were unfounded. She wondered how this information could have reached Mr.

Woodfire.

With a heavy heart, Julie tried to defend herself. "Mr. Woodfire, there must be some misunderstanding. I assure you; My credentials are legitimate. I worked hard to get my master's degree in Denmark."

But Mr. Woodfire was determined. "Miss Goldbucket, we have conducted an internal investigation and there is no doubt about the authenticity of the information we have received. We cannot tolerate dishonesty within our organization."

Julie's mind raced, trying to comprehend what was happening. She had accomplished a lot, and her career had finally reached the pinnacle she had worked tirelessly for. Now, everything was falling apart before her eyes.

"I'm sorry, Miss Julie," Mr. Woodfire went on, "but you don't work for our company anymore. Our attorneys will contact you to discuss your severance package."

The call ended, leaving Julie in shock. She couldn't believe that her dream had vanished so quickly. She had lost her job, and her reputation had been tarnished by false accusations of dishonesty.

Tears welled up in her eyes as she realized that everything, she had worked so hard for so long was slipping out of her hands. The weight of the harsh reality she faced was almost unbearable, and she wondered how she would pick up the pieces and rebuild her life after this devastating blow.

Julie was standing outside the marketing agency, holding a box full of her belongings and trying to process the whirlwind of emotions that had engulfed her. She felt like she was on the verge of a nervous breakdown. The weight of the accusations against her and the sudden loss of her dream job were almost too much to bear.

Tears welled up in her eyes as she looked around, feeling lost and abandoned. She didn't know who to call for support or where to turn. She had dedicated herself to her career, to that company, and now it seemed that everything had been in vain.

As she struggled to regain her composure, Julie finally called her mother, Dinorah. She knew that her mother, a licensed therapist, could offer guidance and emotional support during this difficult time.

Dinorah answered the phone and listened intently as Julie recounted the shocking turn of events. Her mother's reassuring words provided some comfort, though they could not erase the gravity of the situation. Dinorah assured her daughter that they would work things out together and fight to clear her name.

With her mother's support, Julie felt a glimmer of hope. Maybe she could pass this test and prove that she was no liar. The message of "Absolute power does exist" suddenly took on a new meaning. Perhaps she had the power within herself to face this devastating challenge head-on.

Dinorah advised Julie to contact an attorney friend of Barry's and gather any evidence that would help establish the legitimacy of her qualifications. She also encouraged her daughter to reach out to her father, Barry, to get not only his friend's phone number but also his emotional support during this very difficult time.

Julie knew she had to fight for her reputation and her career. She understood that the road ahead would not be easy, but she was not willing to give up, not now. The message about finding answers in nature now seemed more important than ever and, in her mind, she planned a trip to

Marina Willows to find the answers she needed to clear her name and rebuild her life.

Chapter 30: It's Time to Fight Back

The days that followed were super stressful for Julie. She quickly hired Trevor Black, an attorney friend of Barry's, to help her prove the legitimacy of her qualifications and protect her reputation. Together with her lawyer, they began the arduous task of gathering all the evidence to corroborate her academic background and experience.

Julie's father, Barry, proved to be a true, unwavering support during this very difficult period. He listened to her concerns, shared his own life experiences, and offered valuable advice. He reminded Julie that life was full of trials and that setbacks were just opportunities to grow stronger.

Julie's mother, Dinorah, continued to provide emotional support and therapy sessions to help her deal with the stress and anxiety that came with this very challenging situation. Dinorah's guidance helped Julie maintain her composure and focus on the task at hand.

As Julie and her attorney, Mr. Black, delved deeper into her case, they discovered that the allegations against her had originated from a former Human Resources colleague named Hilda, who had recently been fired and with whom she had had issues in the past. This woman had orchestrated the whole plot to tarnish her reputation and get her fired. She apparently changed Julie's documents for fake documents, but they looked very real. It had all started because Hilda had had an affair with Roman, the father of her best friend Maple, many years ago and had contributed to the divorce of her parents. Julie couldn't stand her, there had always been a bad vibe between them and Hilda was jealous of Julie's position. She also disliked her for being Maple's friend. Mr. Black, Julie's attorney, was determined to expose the truth and bring the guilty part to justice.

Amid her legal battle, facing all the stress and anxiety, Julie again remembered that message she had received: "All the answers lie in nature." She took some time off from the case to reconnect with nature and find the inner strength to face the challenges that lay ahead.

Julie returned to Marina Willows, the place where she had discovered the rock painted with the alien symbols and the mysterious numbers, "10:25". She had a hunch that the rock might contain some hidden message or meaning, and she was determined to decipher it.

As she wandered through the park, Julie felt a powerful force calling her to the "Duck Lagoon." Inside the lagoon there was a floating log where three turtles were balancing. She couldn't help but think that perhaps there might be a symbolic connection between the swaying turtles and her current situation.

Julie took a deep breath and sat down on a bench in front of the lagoon, reflecting on the turtles, nature, and the enigmatic messages she had received. Julie was filled with anxiety and understood that the road ahead would not be easy, but she was committed to looking for the answers she needed in nature and restoring her reputation in some way.

Julie was grateful. She had the support of her family and friends, the psychological guidance of her mother, Dinorah, the valuable advice of her father, Barry, and the unbreakable bond with her friend, Maple.

Chapter 31: The Call

Thoughts in her head swirled as she walked alone in the park. Julie dialed her fiancé, Sam's, number. Her heart was beating anxiously, but with determination. She knew this was a pivotal moment, one that would set the trajectory of her life. The phone rang, and with each ring, Julie felt her emotions oscillate between fear and liberation.

Finally, Sam answered the call, with his trademark soft voice. "Hey, Julie, how's everything going? Are you okay?" he asked.

Julie hesitated for a moment; her mind filled with thoughts of all kinds. But she took a deep breath and plucked up the courage to speak her truth. "Sam, we need to talk," Julie said, her voice firm.

There was a brief pause on the other end of the line. Sam's response was tentative but encouraging. "Of course, Julie. What's on your mind? Is everything okay with the lawyer?

Julie didn't think twice and decided to be honest, so she went straight to the point. "Sam, I think it's time for us to take a break. For a long time now, I have been feeling that I am losing myself in this relationship and I need to figure out who I am on my own. I've been dealing with a lot of things, more than you can imagine. Yes, my job is overwhelming, although I always try to seem in control, but I also have my own personal struggles and need some space to figure things out. I think you are a wonderful person and any wom... person would be incredibly lucky to have you as their partner."

There was another pause, this time longer and full of uncertainty.

Sam finally answered; His voice was full of resignation. "Julie, honestly, I've been feeling similar things as well, but I didn't know how to bring it up. I've felt for a while that we've been distancing ourselves; things just aren't the same anymore. I also believe that you are a wonderful woman, and I am sure that you will make the person you choose to be with very happy."

Julie felt a twinge of guilt, but also a sense of relief. She had expected a perhaps more heartbreaking response from Sam, but his willingness to acknowledge the problems in the relationship made her feel like she was making the right decision.

"Sam, this doesn't mean it's the end for us. Maybe taking a break will help us both grow as individuals. Believe it or not, I care a lot about you, and I want the best for both of us," she said in a voice overflowing with sincerity.

Sam agreed and they briefly discussed the logistics of their separation, how they would handle shared belongings, and living arrangements. While it was an emotional and difficult conversation, they both knew it was a necessary step for their personal growth.

Julie hung up the phone with a mix of emotions, but also with a new sense of empowerment. She had taken an important step to get her life back and find the happiness she so deserved. Now, she needed to apply that new inner strength to face her challenges head-on and regain her career and reputation.

Chapter 32: A New Beginning

Julie had made the difficult decision to take a break from her relationship with Sam and that left her feeling incredibly liberated but vulnerable at the same time. As the days passed, Julie faced the challenges of living alone again with Bagel, her cat. The calmness of her penthouse was something different indeed, but refreshing.

She used this time to rediscover herself, her passions, and her sense of purpose. Julie began to try new hobbies such as knitting and painting mandalas on rocks, and she resumed activities that she had neglected for too long, such as riding her bicycle. She took long walks in Marina Willows Park, letting the privileged natural environment calm her thoughts.

One day, while walking near the Serengeti, in the park, she found another of the painted rocks. It had vibrant yellow daffodils in the front and the numbers "11:11" painted on the back. Julie wondered herself what it meant and if this rock had also been painted by Maple, but the truth is that finding it brought a faint smile to her face.

Julie also began spending more time with her parents, Dinorah and Barry. Dinorah offered her guidance and support in the difficult times she faced, while Barry, who had apparently recovered from his heart attack, shared stories from his near-death experience that still baffled and intrigued him.

During this period of introspection, Julie remembered the wisdom of her grandmother, her Nana Minerva, who had once left her with a super wise enigma: "All the answers you seek lie in nature." Julie absorbed this wisdom and found solace in the simplicity of nature. She spent time outdoors, appreciating the beauty of the natural world and she frequently meditated by the hidden lake of Marina Willows Park, in the area not accessible to the public, contemplating the mysteries of life.

One night, Julie received a call from Maple. Julie had been quite worried about her friend, due to her mental health issues. To her delight, Maple's voice sounded firmer and more serene than she had heard in a long time.

"Julie, I wanted to tell you something," Maple began. "I have been living an extraordinary adventure, I have been exploring the realms of the mind, the spirit, nature and the universe. I've met a wonderful being, but I'm not ready to tell you yet. I have found a new sense of balance and happiness within me. And I want to share this adventure with you, if you're willing."

Julie, who had been longing for a deeper sense of purpose, felt a spark of curiosity. She agreed to meet Maple at her apartment the next night.

When she hung up the phone, Julie reflected on her journey of self-discovery. She had taken the first step to regain her independence and now, a new adventure attracted her, one that would lead her to discover her inner power and the secrets hidden in nature. Maple had always been an unusual person, but a very interesting one. Julie was excited to know what Maple was going to tell her.

Julie went to bed that night with a sense of anticipation and hope that her life was taking a new and exciting turn.

Chapter 33: Michael

Julie's life was undergoing a series of profound changes. Her journey of self-discovery led her to face not only her emotions and struggles but also the challenging circumstances of her family members. Michael, her younger brother, had always been the baby of the family. Lately, she had noticed a change in his behavior, the signs of a rebellious teenager facing the complexities of life. For Julie, her brother's well-being was just one of the things she was worried about.

One day, after reconnecting with her own strength and sense of purpose at Marina Willows, Julie decided to reconnect with Michael. She called him and he replied, somewhat surprised by the unexpected call: "Julie, what's wrong? You rarely call me, everything alright?"

Julie felt a surge of love for her little brother when she heard his voice. He didn't sound like a kid anymore, but Julie was determined to let him know how much he meant to her. "Michael," Julie began, "I want you to know something. I love you more than you can imagine, and I will always be here for you, no matter what. I understand that things at your age aren't always easy. When I was your age I had my own dramas. I wanted to fit in. I wanted to be cool. I did a lot of silly things, some of which I regret. But they are part of growing and maturing as a person. I'm sorry, I don't want to bore you."

Michael, surprised by the sincerity of her voice, replied: "You don't bore me, I don't know if you know that, but I love you very much too,

Julie. You've always been there for me and honestly, I've always looked up to you and... I've always been a little envious of you."

With her brother's trust earned, Julie tackled a difficult subject. She knew that sometimes the strongest people were the ones who least sought support when they needed it most. She could see the pain behind Michael's indifferent exterior.

"Michael," Julie whispered, "believe me, there's nothing to envy, as much as it seems like my life is perfect, the truth is that behind the curtain everything is falling apart. Adult life is not easy either. I wanted to talk to you about something and I just want to ask you to listen to me. I've noticed that things have been hard for you lately. You don't have to face those difficulties alone. If you're struggling with something, I want you to know that you can talk to me about anything."

For a moment, there was silence on the other end of the line. Michael hesitated, as if groping the decision to open up to his sister. Then, between nervous stutters, he told her all about his struggles, revealing the terrible weight he had been carrying. He confided in Julie about something very dark that had happened to him a year before in high school, he talked about how his substance abuse problem began and told her about his desire to belong and his fear of disappointing his parents, Dinorah and Barry.

Tears welled up in Julie's eyes as she listened to her brother's vulnerable confession. She understood the magnitude of the moment and the situation. Julie had always been protective of Michael, his older sister, and now he was allowing her into his world, into his struggles, into his pain. Julie assured Michael that her support and love would always be unwavering. She promised him that they would find help together and that their parents would understand and give him the support he needed, that he should not be afraid of them, that they loved him more than he could ever imagine and that his pain was the pain of their parents and the whole family.

"Michael," Julie said, "I want you to really trust me. Let's get through this together. I will help you find the support you need, and we will not let this define your life. I know it sounds cliché, but you have the absolute power to overcome it, and I believe in you. I will always believe in you, and I will always be your big sister."

Michael's voice trembled as he replied, "Julie... Thank you! You don't know how lucky I feel to have you as my sister. I trust you. I promise I will do everything I can to get out of this. I honestly haven't felt good in quite some time with the life I'm leading. I miss being happy...". They continued talking for more than an hour, Julie told him a little about the things she was experiencing as well. Then Julie called her sister Sophie on a teleconference and the three of them talked for a while longer. Sophie was also surprised by the call, but it made her happy. Julie said to the two, "Remember, nothing can stand against the siblinghood!" This conversation marked a before and after in their relationship as siblings, it was a moment of vulnerability and honesty that brought them closer than ever.

Chapter 34: Decisions

The phone rang. Julie was at a crossroads in her life and the decision she made at that moment would define her future. Julie had spent years and years working as a mule to climb the corporate ladder, tirelessly pursuing her dream of becoming a partner at "Irguitzu Marketing Ltd.", the agency where she used to work. However, the truth was that she had been accused of fabricating her credentials, which was unfair, after all her sacrifices. On top of all the stress it had caused her for years, it made her face unexpected adversity.

When the agency's attorney relayed the news that Julie had won the case and offered her a chance to return, Julie's mind raced. But in the moments of silence before her answer, she thought of the unusual message she had received from her Nana Minerva: "Absolute power does exist." Julie had gone through many transformations since she was fired of the agency, rediscovering her own strength and realizing that her true power lay in the choices she made.

Taking a deep breath and feeling a renewed sense of empowerment, Julie decided to step away from the corporate world. She understood that stress, high expectations, and anxiety about success didn't define her. Instead, she would accept the power to shape her own life and follow her own path. Julie's decisive words echoed through the phone, leaving the gentleman in shock. The lawyer paused briefly as he listened to Julie's statements and then told her that he respected her decision.

With her decision already made, Julie decided to lead a life where her well-being, happiness and inner peace would always be above everything else. She was determined to discover a new beginning, making use of the absolute power of her own decisions and living life on her own terms.

Julie hung up the phone, felt everything: relief, liberation, and the excitement of starting over. She was ready to embark on a destination where she would prioritize her own well-being and happiness in order to live the life she had always dreamed of. Julie had an unbreakable spirit and a heart full of hope. There was still much to live for, much to explore in this world full of new opportunities for self-discovery and the search for true satisfaction. The message of the universe had been clear, and Julie was going to follow her own destiny.

Chapter 35: My Best Friend, Maple Pelridge

Without a doubt, Julie had a special bond with her best friend, Maple Pelridge. They had shared countless moments together since childhood, always supporting each other through the ups and downs of life. After her final decision to leave the agency, Julie felt compelled to share the news with Maple. Julie called her and while she told her about the recent changes in her life; the relief she felt at leaving the corporate world behind and especially her separation from Sam, Maple, listened intently.

Maple was super excited about Julie's fresh start and the prospects of self-discovery and fulfillment that lay ahead for her dear friend. She knew how much Julie had longed for this opportunity to escape the constraints of her high-stress job and pursue a new path, free from her meaningless relationship with Sam. Julie also told Maple about her younger brother's struggles with addiction.

Maple, as always, offered her support and empathy to Julie during this difficult period. Maple suggested trying hypnotherapy and also offered to ask for help from her extensive network of followers, which exceeded 3 million, and to use her influence to find the best help available to overcome Michael's addiction.

Maple's rapid rise into the world of online influencers had been her dream for years, and she was finally seeing the magnitude of her power and reach. Julie was grateful to have such a wonderful friend to lean on in those moments, and she was also grateful that Maple was finally reaping the success she had sown with so much love and patience.

Everything had exploded with a simple video that went viral, a video of Maple and her dog Pancake in Marina Willows, a place they both adored. The video showed Pancake running towards Maple after she returned from vacation, licking her entire face. The video was so emotional that it had managed to capture the hearts of millions of viewers around the world, which initiated an avalanche of followers and economic offers for Maple, who really needed it. As Maple shared her sense of humor, her insights, life lessons, and moments of awe with the world, her influence continued to grow exponentially, and she was making a real change on matters that were important to her.

While Julie had always been proud of her friend's talent and her unique perspective on life, she admired the way Maple had harnessed the power of the internet to make a meaningful impact on the world. It was as if the universe had also guided Maple to this new success.

Despite all the challenges in her life and the decision to leave her corporate career behind, as well as ending the relationship with her "perfect" ex-fiancé, Sam, Julie was really happy for Maple. Julie felt that both of her processes of self-discovery were intertwined with the power of something greater, and Maple's happiness was her happiness. When they hung up the phone, Julie felt like she was on the cusp of a new and better destiny.

Leaving the corporate world behind meant discovering her own path to happiness and fulfillment, while Maple was ascending to new heights as an influencer, using her platform to inspire and encourage others. Their friendship was a source of strength, and Julie was excited to see where their newfound power would take them.

Chapter 36: Peace

As Julie sipped the fresh berry smoothie she had made earlier, she couldn't help but marvel at the little joys in life that had taken on new meaning for her. The almost magical whiteness and special sweetness of the berries were like a small burst of happiness in her mouth. Julie had discovered these velvety white berries a few months ago on one of her walks in Marina Willows Park, in a wooded area that people called "Enchanted Forest," but that her friend Maple called "Fairy Forest." Smoothies had become a delicious habit.

With her new free time, Julie had adopted a slower, more relaxed pace of life. The severance package for the dismissal of her old job was quite juicy and provided her with a great sense of financial security, allowing her to enjoy a good period of respite. She was still deciding what her next steps would be, but for the time being, she was content to take life one day at a time.

One day, a deep longing for the ocean had stirred within her. Julie felt an undeniable need to be close to the sea, as if it had the answers to the questions and uncertainties that had piled up in her mind. Leaving her luxurious penthouse, she crossed the street and headed for Marina Willows. The journey to the ocean took her through the heart of the park, through the Serengeti, through Cuervo Hills, through the Duck Lagoon, through the Fairy Forest and along the yellow and white daffodil trail, where she had spent countless hours in reflection and contemplation.

The park had always been like a sanctuary for Julie, a place where she could escape the rigors of her old corporate life and reconnect with the natural world. As she strolled along its criss-crossing paths, her senses came alive with the spectacular sights and mesmerizing sounds of birds, the rustling of leaves on the ground as she walked, and the soft whispers of the wind scurrying through the branches of the trees.

Suddenly, the scent of salt water filled the air and the sound of the waves crashing against the shore grew louder. Julie was getting closer to her destination, the sea. She approached a wooden staircase that led to the beach and, she thought about the meaning of "10:25" as she descended, when she reached the beach, she took off her shoes and felt the sand under her feet and the sea breeze on her face.

When she reached the shore, the magnificent expanse of the ocean stretched out before her. The waves rolled in a rhythmic, almost lethargic pattern. Julie looked at the horizon, watching the sun dance over the surface of the water. The infinite beauty of the sea held her in its embrace, filling her with a sense of calm and wonder.

While Julie stood there, the weight of her past decisions seemed to disappear, if only for a moment. The ocean whispered secrets to her, just as the park had done before. She couldn't explain it, but there was a deep connection between these two places. They offered her a sense of clarity and a reminder that nature had its own wisdom to share.

Julie sat on the shore, feeling the warmth of the sun and the gentle caress of the breeze on her skin. She closed her eyes and listened to the waves, each carrying a message of peace and possibility. The past was behind her, and the future stretched out like the sea waiting to be explored.

In that moment of reflection by the ocean, Julie pondered the power of choosing her own path, of connecting with planet earth, and of following the desires of her dreaming heart.

As she watched the sun slowly dip below the horizon, casting a golden glow on the water, Julie felt an overwhelming sense of gratitude. Something or someone had given her a magnificent gift: the gift of time to rediscover herself and enjoy the beauty and wonders of the world around her.

Chapter 37: Connection

Julie was walking back home through "Cuervo Hills" in Marina Willows, her heart feeling light, and her mind filled with newfound clarity. The stunning beauty of the park, combined with her recent contemplation by the ocean, had helped her rediscover who she really was and made her feel gratitude for the beautiful world around her. Every step she took on the rocky roads felt like a step toward a fuller, more authentic future.

There in Cuervo Hills, she stumbled upon the elegant purple Victorian birdhouse that hung from the sturdy trunk of an old oak tree with twisted branches. A creation of her dear friend Maple, the birdhouse, was a tangible symbol of her creativity and resilience. It was like a reminder that, even amid personal battles, you could create beautiful and special things. Something about Marina Willows had the power to inspire ideas and elevate the mind.

Julie paused to admire the beauty of the Victorian birdhouse. Her thoughts wandered to the nomadic life of birds and their freedom, which she envied. The ability to soar through the skies, free from earthly problems and limitations, was an idea that had always intrigued her.

A gust of wind rustled the leaves of the majestic oak trees above her and sunlight filtered through the branches, drawing figures on the ground. Julie was captivated by the moment and felt a growing desire to share her new perspective and appreciation for life with someone who had always been her source of wisdom and guidance.

She reached into her purse, pulled out her latest-model PiPhone with the cracked screen, and dialed her father's number. Barry had always been a pillar of strength in her life, and Julie wanted to connect with him and share the details of the transformation she was experiencing within her being.

The phone rang and Julie waited anxiously for the other end to connect. She heard her father's sweet voice on the line. "My beautiful little girl!" he said, in an affectionate tone.

"Daddy," Julie began, her voice full of excitement and happiness, "I just wanted to talk to you, share the wonderful things that have been happening to me for a while now."

Barry listened intently, his wisdom waiting to give his advice while encouraging Julie to share her experiences and her views. Julie told him a little more in detail about the enigmas that had appeared in her life, from her Nana Minerva's words about "Absolute Power" to her recent reconnection with nature and the new freedom she was discovering away from the corporate world.

As she spoke, Barry's own supernatural experiences with other levels of existence came to the forefront of his mind. He had already shared with his daughter that moment of transcendence, that journey towards the light that had taken him to the edge of another world and back. Although he hadn't revealed to Julie the entirety of his experiences, talking about such strange and special topics created a unique connection between Julie and Barry to the mysterious and unexplained vast universe in which we float.

Barry shared stories of his own spiritual awakening, the path of multicolored light he had followed, and the presence of beings both known and unknown to him that he had encountered along the way. Many of the beings he encountered in the light were his ancestors. Although they did not speak to him, he communicated with those beings from within, without the use of words. He saw all the pets he had ever had throughout his life and had wordless conversations with them. It was a story he had kept to himself, afraid of what others might think, but at that moment he felt a deep connection to his daughter Julie and enough confidence to talk about such topics.

Julie was moved to realize that her father had also found answers and comfort in the unexplained. Sharing their stories created a bond that transcended the ordinary, strengthening the connection between them even more.

As the conversation continued, the feeling of gratitude and love for her father grew. He had always been there for her, offering guidance and support throughout her life. She hung up the phone, with a sense of inner peace and satisfaction.

With every step she took on her way home, the echoes of her conversation with her beloved father reverberated within her. The birdhouse, the trees, the animals, the natural world around her, all were a constant reminder of the beauty of life.

Chapter 38: Goodbye

Four days after Julie's conversation with her father, Barry Goldbucket, a man who had been a guiding light in her life, took his last breath and departed this world. The news struck Julie and the family like lightning, leaving them caught up in sadness and disbelief.

Barry's passing was a profound loss, not only to his immediate family but also to the countless lives he had touched throughout his time in this world. As an accountant, he had provided financial stability and advice to many individuals and businesses, earning the trust and respect of those he had worked with.

Julie's mother, Dinorah, was perhaps the one who suffered the most from her loss. Barry was her rock, her everything. Despite the pain, she kept her family together with strength and grace, just as Barry had done during his life. Barry had been a loyal and devoted husband to Dinorah, a loving father to Julie, Sophie, and Michael, and a dear friend to many. Barry was always a source of advice for everyone who knew him.

The sudden loss of her father, a man she had always admired, respected, and loved, absolutely devastated Julie. In the midst of her pain, she recalled those conversations they had shared throughout her life. She recalled her trips to the countryside, the mountains and the beach as a child, his sense of humor and the silly dad jokes he would make. Julie also thought about the deep connection they had formed in his last days. Those mystical conversations were a fantastic, unexpected farewell, one she would treasure forever.

The days that followed were filled with a lot of preparations and visits. The entire extended family gathered to honor and remember Barry; his sisters, cousins, nephews, and people Julie didn't even know shared stories and memories of her father's life. The outpouring of support from friends and family was like a small glimmer of comfort during that very difficult time.

Despite many family members disagreeing, Barry was cremated and scattered on his favorite mountain. Among the mountains, friends and family gathered to celebrate Barry's life and offer their condolences. There was a sense of sadness in the air, but of gratitude for this fleeting life, between tears and smiles. The stories that his loved ones shared were a sign of what a great human being, Barry Goldbucket was.

When Julie stood in front of the family and others who came to offer their condolences, she found the strength to share the story of her recent conversations with her father. She did not speak of the messages from the afterlife, but she did speak of the intense connection they had forged in the last few days and the sense of peace and understanding that had permeated the depths of her being in those moments. Julie's every word was like a tribute to the deep and enduring connection she had with her father, even beyond the borders of this world.

In the days that followed, as the family found their way forward, the pain of loss became a little more tolerable. The memory of Barry would live on in their hearts.

While the three siblings, Julie, Sophie and Michael, collected Barry's old belongings, they saw photos of his youth, of his travels, of the romance with Dinorah, the births of his children. The siblings connected in a way they hadn't in years. Suddenly, Julie's younger sister, Sophie, who had just come back from her vacation in Southeast Asia with her boyfriend, found a small notebook that appeared to be a diary. The diary did not appear to be her father's. Sophie inspected it and said: "! It's from Nana Minerva!"

Julie heard this and got excited; she told Sophie to pass it to her. Julie opened it randomly on a page marked July 11, 1946.

"Good morning to my body and soul! Today is another beautiful day, but here I am, sleepy, yet sleepless. I think about a lot of things, especially those I can't control. What can I control? I can control my limits, but then... What are my limits? Maybe I don't have limits. Limitless... Love without limits... Does it exist? What is love without limits? All I know is that the only thing that matters is rule number one. You have to have fun, and the only real fun comes from love. I am a product of love and fun and more love, therefore, I am made of love and fun.

Can I have true love without rule number one? The answer is no. Can you be truly successful at anything without rule number one? The answer is no. So, I ask myself: What's the point of life, if it's not fun? Well, life is precious, but without fun, it has no meaning and without love; it is not life.

Love is everything, and everything is love. Once you find love, no matter how hard you try, you will never let go and love will never let go of you. Love comes in all shapes and all colors. Each color is the color of Love. I just showered. I feel like a new person. After all, water is the essence of life. It is composed of different elements but flows as one.

All I know is that life is strange. Will I ever be really happy? Could it be that absolute power exists? The power to take my destiny into my own hands."

As Julie read it, her siblings were excited to get to know their beloved grandmother a little more in depth and Julie felt a little comfort at the thought that Barry was finally reunited with his mother, Minerva.

The man-shaped tree with his arms raised in Marina Willows, and the Victorian-style birdhouse in Cuervo Hills, the site of Julie's last conversation with Barry, for some strange reason became symbols of remembrance of their beloved father and a tangible connection to the afterlife.

Losing a loved one is an experience that forever changes a person's life. Julie, Dinorah, Michael, Sophie and their family found themselves more united than ever by the enduring memory of a man who had had a profound impact on their lives.

As life progressed, the deep feeling of gratitude for the moments she had shared with her father only grew stronger. Barry Goldbucket's passing marked the end of an era in Julie's life, but the nature of the human spirit is eternal.

Chapter 39: Spirituality

Julie's world had changed forever after her father's passing. She was no longer the same woman who had walked through life, focusing singularly on her career and her material success. The messages from the afterlife and the deep connection she had shared with her father had opened her eyes to a deeper understanding of life, death, and the mysteries of the universe.

As Julie mourned her father's death, she found herself drawn to spirituality. She explored the spiritual teachings that resonated with her, seeking comfort and wisdom in the belief that life extended beyond the physical world. Her father, Barry, had been a man of deep spiritual understanding, and she felt a desire to continue his legacy of seeking greater truths.

Julie delved into books and teachings about life after death, reincarnation, and the interconnectedness of all living things. She attended meditation and mindfulness sessions, allowing herself to be present in the moment and open her arms to the beauty of nature, just as her grandmother, Nana Minerva, had suggested in her message from the afterlife.

Marina Willows became a truly sacred space for Julie, a place of reflection, connection, and remembrance. It was there that she often walked through "Cuervo Hills," where the crows squawked as if they were conversing with beings from beyond. The Victorian birdhouse that Maple had created was a symbol of the intricate relationship between the physical and spiritual worlds, a constant reminder of her father's presence.

Julie cherished her conversations with her mother, Dinorah, who had also been deeply affected by Barry's passing. Mother and daughter found comfort in their shared grief and in their exploration of spiritual concepts. Together, they discussed the mysteries of the universe, messages from the afterlife, and the belief that life was a balance between joy and sadness. Dinorah, as a psychologist, had her feet well on this ground, but conversations with her patients had opened her mind about the possibilities of other dimensions of reality and existence.

Dinorah, with her experience, offered Julie a unique perspective on healing and spiritual growth. She introduced Julie to various spiritual practices, including mindfulness meditation, which provided a sense of inner peace and connection to the unknown.

Julie opened her arms to her evolving spirituality. Everything resonated with the messages she had received: "Absolute power does exist" and "All answers lie in nature." She realized that absolute power was not about control or dominance, but about the innate power within each person to create their own reality. The answers in nature uncovered the interconnectedness of all life, the wisdom one could find in the natural world, and the understanding that we are all part of a greater everything.

Her father's passing had ignited a spiritual awakening within Julie. She learned to find beauty in the balance of life's dualities, accepting both light and darkness, joy and sadness. She discovered that her connection to her father transcended the physical world, and he was still alive in her heart and in the life lessons he had given her.

In this chapter of her life, Julie was no longer defined by her career or her material things. Now it would be defined by her inner discovery, her spiritual growth, and the realization that love and connection could encompass the boundaries of life and death. The exploration of Julie's spirituality was like a tribute to her father and a source of strength as she continued to navigate the complexities of existence.

Julie had kept her Nana Minerva's diary and one day she was curious to read another page. She opened it on a page marked February 23, 1954.

"Today is the first day of the rest of my life! Today is the day I realized that I know everything, but I know nothing. I wonder why life is so simple yet so complicated. Today I choose to be happy, even if it means that others won't understand it, after all, the only rule that matters is number one: "You must have fun", but one could say, having fun can get you in trouble... Well, I say, sometimes you have to get into a little trouble if you want to enjoy life, after all... How will we know which rules are correct and which are not? Sometimes we have to defy the rules to be able to find out if everything we've learned is a big lie and the only rule that matters is number two: Do everything with and for love."

Chapter 40: Metamorphosis

Julie's life had undergone a profound transformation since her father's death. She had let go of the corporate world, choosing to follow a simpler path that resonated with her heart's desires. High-paying, high-stress work was no longer her priority. Instead, she took a job at the local bookstore, immersing herself in the world of literature and surrounded by the wisdom of countless authors.

The job at the bookstore paid a modest salary, but Julie had never been happier. She was finally living a life that aligned with her true passions and values. With her father's guidance from the afterlife and the lessons she had learned along the way, Julie understood that she could measure the richness of life not by the size of her paycheck, but by the depth of her experiences and connections.

Her new job allowed her to meet a wide range of people, each with their own unique stories and interests. Julie was able to share her knowledge and enthusiasm for literature, helping clients find books that sparked their imaginations and offered new perspectives.

In her spare time, which was a lot more now, Julie continued to explore her spirituality. She spent more time at Marina Willows, deepening her connection to nature. She found comfort in the wisdom of the crows, was inspired by the ever-changing colors of the sky during sunset and heard the songs of the wind rustling through the trees. She realized that nature was the supreme teacher.

Julie's life had been simplified, but it had also been enriched in meaning. She no longer measured her success by external standards, but by the love and connections she had cultivated. She was more in tune with herself, with her values and with her desires.

Julie's newfound simplicity allowed her to rediscover the joy of everyday life. She enjoyed the simple pleasures: a hot cup of tea on a rainy day, the smell of a freshly opened book, and the comfort of her cozy home. She had taken the time to nurture her relationship with Bagel, addressing his dental issues.

While Julie had chosen a life that many would consider modest, she felt incredibly rich in the things that mattered most: love, connection, self-discovery, and a new sense of inner peace. She had found happiness in simplicity and fulfillment in the pursuit of her true passions.

As she lay on her king-size bed, enjoying the tranquility of her new life, playing "Fruit Smasher" on her PiPhone, Julie couldn't help but smile. She was grateful for her father's guidance from the afterlife, the unwavering support of her mother, Dinorah, the improved relationship with her siblings Sophie and Michael, and of course, Maple's unwavering friendship. She was grateful for the lessons learned along her journey of self-discovery, for the messages that had led her to accept the absolute power within herself.

Julie knew her life had come full circle, and when she closed her eyes to meditate, she felt an overwhelming sense of satisfaction and gratitude. She lived a simple, beautiful, and deeply fulfilling life, a life that was entirely her own.

The end.

Glossary

Julie Marie Goldbucket: The protagonist of the story, a dedicated marketing professional who seeks success and fulfillment in a beautiful small town in the Pacific Northwest

Dr. Dinorah Goldbucket: Julie's mother, a psychologist, who offers perspective and guidance.

Barry Goldbucket: Julie's beloved father, who offers advice and unconditional support.

Michael Goldbucket: Julie's younger brother, struggles with addiction.

Sophie Goldbucket: Julie's younger sister, living her own life carefreely.

Nana Minerva: Julie's deceased grandmother, who imparts profound messages to Julie throughout the story.

Maple Pelridge: Julie's best friend, deeply connected to nature and the universe, possibly going through a mental health episode.

Sam: Julie's fiancé, whose preferences spark doubts in Julie.

Mr. Thomas Woodfire: The CEO of Julie's former marketing agency, Irguitzu Marketing Ltd.

Ramon Chespirito: Executive Director of "Verypech" cuaba soaps, for the Latin American marketing account.

Grisell: Mr. Woodfire's Secretary

Joan: Partner of Irguitzu Inc., bootlicker par excellence.

Hilda: Julie's former colleague, a woman with whom Maple's father, Roman, had an affair.

Trevor Black: Julie's lawyer, a friend of her father, Barry.

Benjie: Julie's assistant.

Bagel: Julie's cat.

Marina Willows: Julie's favorite spot, a huge park on the edge of her city.

Fairy Forest: A nickname Julie's friend, Maple, invented for a lush, wooded area of Marina Willows with a charming energy.

The Serengeti: A nickname Julie's friend, Maple, invented for a part of Marina Willows; it conjures up images of the African plains in documentaries.

Cuervo Hills: Immersed in the Serengeti, deep in Marina Willows.

The Duck Lagoon: A part of Marina Willows, where Julie sees three turtles swinging on a floating log.

Sky Water: Musical group.

Notes:

Absolute power does exist!

104